I0536204

CORNERED

"Take it easy, sister," the man with the glasses told her. Just be a good girl and you won't get hurt."

"If it's money you want . . ." Nancy said.

"Not money, honey. Just relax."

THE IMPETUOUS MISTRESS

"California has its ERLE STANLEY GARD-NER and New York its ELLERY QUEEN, but Connecticut can claim GEORGE HARMON COXE for the most top-flight mystery writer in the business"

—*Bridgeport Sunday Post*

THE IMPETUOUS MISTRESS

GEORGE HARMON COXE

WILDSIDE PRESS

FOR

George Coxe Frazier

THE IMPETUOUS MISTRESS

1

THE HEAT WAVE which came unfailingly to blanket the eastern shore at least once each summer descended with the advent of August and was still going strong five days later. Those who could get out of the cities did so. Those who could not leave, complained, tempers became frayed, the near-by beaches and the roads feeding them were jammed over the week end, and cold drinks were consumed in record quantitites.

Rick Sheridan was one of the lucky ones who had been able to escape on the first day, which was a Thursday. He had driven out to this small house he had recently finished across the Connecticut line with two roughs for what would one day be page advertisements for True-Fruit, a soft drink that had hopes of emulating Pepsi-Cola in popularity, promising his agent that he would deliver the finished art on Tuesday morning.

Because he had insisted on using plenty of insulation, the house stayed comfortable until midafternoon and he had worked steadily on Friday and Saturday. Sunday he had loafed, spending much of his time at the beach, and by Monday noon his two illustrations were ready and he was in excellent spirits, not only because he felt his work was good but because he had telephoned Nancy Heath in New York and she had agreed to take the train to Westport, have dinner with him, and drive back to the city that evening.

There was no hint of the trouble that was to come until the telephone began to ring that afternoon. The first call came from his agent at a quarter of four, just as he was about to stop work on the portrait of Elinor Farrell, who sat near the big studio window.

"Hey, Rembrandt," Ted Banks said. "Tomorrow's Tuesday."

"Yeah," said Rick. "August sixth."

"How're you and True-Fruit doing?"

5

"We're done. Finished this noon."

"Ahh. You're my boy. What do you think?"

"I think it's pretty good."

"It better be because I've been making a big pitch. The client likes your stuff and if they go for these two we get thirteen-fifty for the next job."

"I love you."

"I love you, too. Just be here by ten in the morning."

Rick turned away, pleased with the good news and grinning absently until his glance touched the portrait. He surveyed it critically as he cleaned a brush.

"That's about it, Elinor," he said.

"You mean it's finished?"

"No, I mean for today."

"Oh, dear." Elinor Farrell sighed. "I was hoping—but you'll surely have it Friday. It has to be framed, too . . . Could I see it now, please?"

Rick smiled at her as he carefully reversed the canvas on the easel and carried it over to one wall. "I'd rather you didn't," he said. "It's always better to see a picture for the first time in a frame, even if it isn't the perfect frame. And you'll have it Friday. But I'd like to think about it another day or so. Maybe it's all right now but if you could come Wednesday, just in case I want to touch it up here and there."

He knew she was giving the portrait to her husband as a present. He did not know what the occasion was but the private unveiling was to be on Friday and he was satisfied now that the job could be done on time.

"You'll probably have some fault to find anyway," he said. "Austin, too. People usually do, especially the immediate family."

"Well, we won't have to worry about that," Elinor said. "And if it is anywhere near as good as the one you did of Greta Lane two years ago I know I'll be delighted."

Rick remembered the other portrait because he had not done one since. For although he had the facility of catching a likeness, he did not like the work because there were usually so many changes to be made that he felt the result was a patchwork that took much too long to complete. In this case he needed the fifteen hundred Elinor would pay. He had spent too much on the house, and too much of his own time helping the workman, and the fee would go a long way toward taking care of the first year at Exeter for his son, Ricky, now at camp in the Adirondacks.

This portrait was a sitting pose and he had an interesting subject. For at forty-two Elinor Farrell was a handsome, intelligent woman who might have been beautiful had it not been for the pain and suffering which had become ingrained in her face and had been put there by an accident that nearly cost her life.

The collision between the convertible and the tractor truck had broken three of Austin Farrell's ribs and a leg. His wife, with hardly a scratch on her, had suffered a serious brain injury. An emergency operation by a neurosurgeon had saved her, but there remained a partial paralysis of one leg, a paralysis that was to become gradually worse, and with no hope of eventual recovery.

These things showed in her face, but there was a serenity, too, and no sign of self-pity in her smile or in her words. The well-spaced brown eyes reflected dignity and courage, and the once brown hair, now nearly gray, was softly waved and worn low at the sides to hide the ugly scar above one ear where the blood-clot had been removed.

"In a pinch," Rick said, "I can lend you a frame for Friday. I have one that size and you can use it until you find one you think is right."

The ring of the telephone forestalled any reply, and when he had excused himself and crossed the room the crisp, assertive voice of his wife came to him.

"Rick? Frieda."

"Yes, Frieda."

"I've been thinking about that matter we discussed last week. Do you still want it?"

"The divorce? Certainly I want it."

"Well, maybe it can be arranged."

"I'm glad you changed your mind."

"There'll be some stipulations but nothing insurmountable. How about this evening?"

"Fine," Rick said and then, remembering Nancy Heath: "but I've got a dinner date."

"With the girl friend?"

"Does it matter?"

"I don't suppose it does, actually. As a matter of fact I'm having dinner with Father and I thought I could drive over afterwards. Say around nine."

Rick hesitated but not for long. He was not sure what he would do about Nancy but this was too important to miss.

"Nine o'clock? Okay, I'll be here."

"Good . . . 'Bye."

He stood for a few moments after he had replaced the instrument, a new kind of hope rising in him as he realized what a divorce could mean. Then, before he moved away, the telephone jangled for the third time and when he picked it up he heard the voice of Tom Ashley, his next door neighbor.

"How about dinner tonight?"

"I'm sorry, Tom, but Nancy's coming out."

"Oh. Well, how about bringing her over later?"

"I can't do that either," Rick said and spoke of his wife. "She's having dinner with her father and then she's coming over to talk about a divorce."

"Ahh. Good enough. That's what you want, isn't it? You think she'll go along?"

"That's what I'm hoping."

"Okay then. But if you and Nancy want to stop for a quick one before dinner I'll be here."

Rick thanked him again and hung up, and now as he turned away he heard the car stop out front. He glanced at Elinor and smiled.

"I guess that's Austin," he said, and stepped over to get the crutch that rested in the corner.

She had pulled herself from the chair as he came to her and now she offered her right hand in a formal handshake which was a customary part of each arrival and departure. He stepped back then, aware that she did not want to be helped, and walked with her across the living room to the front door.

A heavy hardtop, shiny, new-looking, and dark-hued, stood in the drive, and when Austin Farrell saw them he stepped down, a tall and handsome figure clad in light-weight doeskin trousers and a dark-blue polo shirt with his initials on the pocket. Two or three years younger than his wife and a confirmed bachelor until their marriage some years earlier, he was a literary agent who worked when he felt like it and practiced his business not for profits—his wife was a wealthy woman who indulged him generously—but for the prestige he felt such labors gave him. As an agent he had a certain standing with the sort of people he felt were important; he had entree to the proper clubs and restaurants where his entertaining was done. For himself he needed only to earn spending money since all other things were signed for to be taken care of by his wife's business manager. Now he smiled to show his perfect teeth, and his voice was low and resonant as he spoke.

"How did it go today, darling?"

"Rick says it's about finished," she said, handing him her crutch as he helped her onto the front seat, "but he'd like another look Wednesday."

"Fine. That's great. I can't wait to see it."

"No literary work today, Austin?" Rick said.

"In this heat?" Farrell laughed. "Try and find an editor in town. I'm going in tomorrow though, just in case. What about you?"

"I'm driving in later this evening. Some stuff to deliver in the morning. . . . I'll phone you Wednesday morning, Elinor, and we can fix a time. It shouldn't take long."

He watched the big car pull away and then went back to the studio to clean up his things, glancing again with satisfaction at the two illustrations he created for True-Fruit out of paint, illustration board, and a penciled rough an art director had furnished him.

He recalled the raise Ted Banks had mentioned and allowed himself to speculate with some pleasure on the future. The hope that had come to him with his wife's call was still with him, but it was a hope tempered with vague misgivings when he remembered the explosive scenes that had erupted between them in times past. What, he wondered, did Frieda mean by certain stipulations?

The thought still lay dormant in the back of his mind when he saw Nancy Heath step down from the 6:48. In that moment before she saw him he watched her move with grace along the station platform, some odd chemical suddenly working on him to set up the pleasurable and exciting currents that always vibrated inside him when he was with her.

She saw him then and waved, her step quickening, a tallish girl in an off-white, tropical-weight suit that still looked fresh after the train ride. Slenderly made but not thin, she had shapely legs and a small neat waist and hair that was medium blond. Her smile came quickly, and when she stopped and he took her hands, he wanted very much to kiss her right then and there. The wide green eyes beneath the dark lashes had soft, humorous lights in them as they held his briefly, telling him that she wanted to be kissed. Then the moment passed and they were walking to his car and he was saying:

"How did it go today?"

"Hectic as usual. If it hadn't been for the air conditioning the whole office would have perished. Did you finish the True-Fruit pages?"

"Yep. Had a session with Elinor Farrell this afternoon and I think I've about done it." He opened the car door and moved round to the other side. "It should be a bit cooler by the water. What about some cold lobster?"

"Oh, perfect," she said delightedly. "With mayonnaise and potato chips and a salad and maybe iced tea."

The place Rick took her to did not have much style but the porch where one dined in the summer jutted out over the water and the lobsters were superb. Because they were reasonably early Rick managed a table by the railing and not until their drinks had been served did he mention his wife.

"She phoned about four," he said. "She wants to see me tonight."

"Ohh—" Nancy's mouth was round with the word and her lips stayed parted until she had digested the news. "But you could have called me, darling," she said. "I didn't have to come out for dinner. I mean, seeing her is so much more important—"

"I'm not meeting her until nine."

"Well—you can put me on the train first."

"No. I've got to drive in anyway." He reached out to cover her hand with his. "Relax," he said. "Just drop me at the house at five of nine, cruise around for three quarters of an hour or so, and then pick me up."

She finished her drink as the waiter put the split lobster before her. She said: "Um," and attacked it with gusto. She muttered small delighted sounds as she ate, smiling at him from time to time as she noted his progress. Not until she had finished did her face sober.

"Do you think she'll give it to you?"

"She called me up," Rick said.

"Last week she said no."

"Maybe she changed her mind."

"Maybe." She sighed as she used the finger bowl. "But I can't see Frieda giving you anything unless it was to her advantage. What exactly did she say?"

"She asked me if I still wanted a divorce, and I said yes, and she said maybe it could be arranged. There might be a couple of stipulations but nothing—to use her word— insurmountable."

"There would be stipulations."

"So what? She probably wants to have an agreement about Ricky."

"I don't know why she should. She's never paid any attention to him."

"She has her rights, too. Her father would like nothing better than to have Ricky with him, and when Frieda has custody she can do as she likes about that. . . . Look," he said with affectionate bluntness. "We want to get married and have a family of our own and live together the next eighty or ninety years, don't we?"

"Well, fifty anyway," she said and giggled.

"And unless I get the divorce it doesn't happen. Who cares what she wants?"

"But you can't give her a mortgage on the rest of your life."

"How do you know she wants a mortgage? I don't intend to give her anything that should be yours."

"I didn't mean that—"

"And anyway, she's got money. I have to scratch all year to make as much as she gets from her mother's estate. I expect to educate Ricky. If she'll settle for a divorce she can have what she wants."

"Within reason."

"Okay, baby. Within reason."

"All right, darling. I'm sorry to be so female about it." She put aside her napkin and her eyes were softly mischievous. "Isn't it nearly time to go? I want to be kissed."

She waited until they were in the car and then, as his arm moved round her, she came close and clung to him while their lips met. When she released herself she straightened and sighed happily.

"Umm," she said. "I feel better already."

It was dark by the time they approached the house. Diagonally across from it was a small lane that was usually occupied during the summer by one car or another and for a purpose which to Rick seemed obvious. Lover's Lane was what he called it privately and though he was vaguely aware that it was presently in use he was more intent on his own driveway and now he noted with relief that there was no sign of Frieda's car. As he stepped out and Nancy moved behind the wheel he said:

"You know your way around most of these roads, but don't get lost."

She said she would try not to. She said she would be back in forty-five minutes and if Frieda's car was parked out front she would drive round again.

"Right," he said. "Just keep your fingers crossed and think positive thoughts. I'll handle Frieda."

2

WHEN Rick Sheridan had turned on some lights in the living room he saw that the clock on the mantel said it was five minutes of nine, and suddenly he was no longer so sure of himself. A new nervousness was working on him, and when he realized he was pacing back and forth he went to the kitchen and brought back the brandy bottle and two miniature snifter glasses.

He poured a tot and swallowed it slowly and by then he could face the fact that during the past several years Frieda had become rather difficult for anyone to handle. She was no longer the girl he had married but, viewed honestly, he was not the same man either. Fourteen years was a long time. He was twenty then, finishing his junior year at college and the war was yet to be won. Frieda was six months older and eager for the elopement that would take her away from the dominating ways of a father who had wanted a son and insisted on treating her like one. What he had to face now as he heard the car stop outside was a self-centered and officious business woman with a calculating mind and a conscience she could turn on and off whenever she found it troublesome.

"Hello," she said as he opened the door for her. "I didn't see your car."

"Nancy has it."

There was no reply to this as she stopped just beyond the entrance to examine the room she had never seen before. "You're quite cozy here. Do you still play?" She indicated the battered upright in one corner and Rick said: "Yes," because he knew what she meant.

In college he had belonged to a small, informal singing group that had no connection with the glee club. Its primary aim, aside from close harmony, was social, and they sang mostly for those whose wealth and position made it possible to put them up for the night or the week end. There were always girls and always there was a time when

13

the piano became the center of attraction. Rick was no musician but he had a nice way with a piano. His left hand was better than most, he had a good memory for melody once exposed to it, and he could fake a fair accompaniment. Frieda liked to sing. . . .

He closed his mind to such thoughts and watched her move round the perimeter of the room, examining this and that and stopping for a moment or two before the framed samples of his work on the walls.

He waited, inspecting the simple white dress and the scarf which had contained her blond hair and now hung knotted about her neck. On the tall side, she no longer had the softly curving figure he once knew so well. Instead she had acquired the planes and angles that characterized the sleek and curveless bodies of the high-fashion models currently in vogue. Her facial make-up was perfection itself, her tan was smooth and even, her manner superior even in repose. This, Rick knew, was a woman who knew what she wanted, and for a long time now it had not been him. He saw she was again looking at the piano and now she said:

"Same two keys?"

"C and G?" He grinned then, surprised that she should remember. "Just the same. More clinkers now though because I don't practice much. . . . Would you like a drink?"

She looked at him then, her blue eyes steady. She shook her head. "Not now, thanks." She sat down on the edge of the divan and crossed brown legs. She put her expensive-looking straw bag on one knee and propped her elbow on the bag.

"About this divorce business," she said, all business now. "I've been thinking. Until now the separation agreement we have has done well enough. You want to marry the Heath girl. I haven't any immediate plans but I might have some day so maybe it's not such a bad idea. Just what do you propose?"

Such phrasing disconcerted Rick because he had not been prepared for it. He sat down opposite her, a frown puckering his brows and his brown eyes uncertain.

"What do you mean, propose?"

"Well, there has to be some agreement, doesn't there? Some meeting of the minds?"

"I thought—" Rick hesitated, recalling the one page separation agreement they had signed more than two years earlier. "Unless you're talking about alimony—"

"I shan't need alimony."

"Then what's wrong with the agreement we have? I'll educate Ricky and pay whatever you think I should for his support."

"That's all well and good but the custody terms will have to be revised."

"Oh?"Rick remembered her reference to stipulations and now he felt a mounting uneasiness that was akin to fear. "Why?"

She shrugged one shoulder and her brow arched. "Because I don't think it's equitable. My time for having Ricky is when he's in school. You have him for vacations."

"He was always in school of one sort or another even when we lived together."

"That's beside the point. I want the vacation time."

"You or your father?"

"Don't quibble, Rick."

Rick sat down opposite her, his throat dry and an unwonted anger beginning to stir inside him.

"All right, Frieda. What exactly do you want?"

"I want Ricky. I want custody. So he can be with me—or Father, if you insist—when I want him."

He stared at her an incredulous moment, hearing the cool concise phrasing and understanding every syllable. Yet even then he could not accept the statement. She had not moved, and her small face was smooth and unlined. Except for the fact that she was not dressed for the city she might have been sitting in her office discussing a book contract with a writer, as befitted her position as a partner in the book publishing firm of Brainard & Eastman—Brainard being her maiden name.

"Oh, no, Frieda," he said.

"Naturally you'll have reasonable visitation rights."

"When it's convenient for you."

"Those are your words, not mine."

He took a breath and glanced at the brandy bottle. He had to work this out without stripping his emotional gears, and yet he knew he could not match her assurance and present self-control because she was talking contracts and rights and he was talking about a twelve-year-old, towheaded boy who was never very far from his thoughts, a boy who returned his love and admiration and still thought his father was a real great guy.

He tried again, unaware that his inflection was growing caustic, not knowing that what he considered simply a lack of affection for his wife was in reality a well-developed dislike.

"Since when have you taken all this interest in motherhood?"

For the first time annoyance flickered in her blue eyes.

"What do you mean by that? I *am* his mother."

"You bore him, if that's what you mean. But what about the other things a child needs? He was three months old when I got back from France and even then you had a full-time nurse."

"Why not? I could afford it then. Does that imply—"

He cut her off because the things in his mind could no longer go unsaid.

"Once he stopped being a baby how many times did you tuck him in bed or listen to his prayers or read to him or tell him stories? It was always me or the nurse, wasn't it? From the time he could toddle you had him in nursery school. He came home to a nurse. You didn't have the time; you couldn't be bothered—"

"Oh, shut up!"

He stood up, avoiding her glance, knowing that her temper, like his, was getting frayed and unpredictable. He stepped to the table and poured some brandy into the glass, swished it absently and gulped it as if it were water.

Still holding the glass he stared out the window into the night, a moderately tall man with a lanky, loose-muscled look and straight dark hair that was sometimes stubborn. His brows were straight and black over the brooding brown eyes and his bony face was tight above the solidly set jaw. In those silent moments there was no outward movement of his body except the uncontrollable tremor in his hands, but he could feel the stiffness in his knees and an internal shakiness that spread out from the pit of his stomach. Finally he put the glass aside and turned back to his wife.

"Why, Frieda?" he asked, trying to keep his voice steady.

"Why what?"

"The sudden possessiveness about Ricky? Because you know a divorce is important to me and you want to be vindictive—though God knows why you should be? Or is this your father's idea? Does he want to mold the boy the way he tried to mold you?"

She had herself in hand again and her voice was clipped. "Do you think you and Nancy can give him a better home than Dad and I?"

He started to ask her just how often she expected to be at home and then reconsidered because her question had merit. Twice Nancy had driven with him to camp to see the boy and they had quickly formed a mutual admiration society. This much he knew, just as he knew that in his daydreams the past few months he had seen Ricky and Nancy in this house together; he had even planned the layout so that an extra room or two could easily be added.

"Perhaps not in material things," he said. "But one thing we could give him that your father has never been capable of, and that is understanding and affection. . . . No," he said as he moved away from the table. "No deal. Visitation rights are not enough, Frieda."

"Very well." She tucked her bag under her arm and straightened her back. "In that case you and Miss Heath will have to accustom yourselves to the idea of sleeping together without benefit of clergy. Not that you haven't already tried it."

He started for her as she finished; then stopped as she jumped to her feet to face him. The words that came to him died in his throat as a cold fury possessed him. In that instant he hated this woman and the cold bright glints in her eyes told him that hate was returned. He made one more effort to preserve his self-control.

"Then let's fight it out the other way. There's one ground for divorce in New York State, so let's see whose skirts are clean."

"What do you mean?" she demanded, and for that instant her glance wavered. "Are you—"

"I mean I've heard things here and there and if this is the way you want it I'll get some private detective and find out how accurate the rumors are. Let's see what a judge will say about this custody business once the facts are in."

"Try it!" she shouted, her voice shrill. "Just you try it."

"I intend to," he yelled, and took a breath, standing with his face no more than a foot from hers, seeing the ugly distortion of her features and knowing his own expression must be equally twisted and stiff. "And if your conduct the past couple of years hasn't been one hundred per cent virginal—which I damned well doubt—"

She hit him then, an open-handed, swinging blow that caught him on the cheekbone, and for the first time in his life he retaliated.

There was no thought process involved. At that moment he was beyond thinking. He felt the sting of the blow and instantly his own hand moved in an instinctive reflex action, as automatic as a skilled boxer counterpunching.

He saw her head rock as his palm caught her cheek, watched her stagger off balance and sit down on the edge of the divan and then skid off to the floor. She landed in a sitting position and there she stayed, more bewildered than hurt, her mouth open and her eyes incredulous.

For a long and silent moment as the shock immobilized them he stared down at her, horrified, the sickness rising in him as he realized what had happened. Then he wheeled and headed for the door as she found her voice.

The screams that followed him were hysterical, the words incoherent. He kept his eyes on the door, not daring to look back. Somehow he knew that if he listened or hesitated or tried to argue again the fury that possessed him might drive him to further violence.

It was fear that drove him on, the certain knowledge that he must get away before it was too late. He reached the door and stumbled into the night and the screams were muted. He passed the convertible and found the highway and turned left, his mind still tormented and the sickness rising in his throat.

He was vaguely aware that next door Tom Ashley's house was dark and the garage empty. He was conscious enough of his surroundings to move to the side of the road when he heard an approaching car. He walked fast, driving himself in an effort to steady his nerves and erase the physical shakiness that still gripped him. When, finally, he could begin to think again he began to ask questions, some of them aloud.

Why? What happened that he could do such a thing?

Never before had he ever touched his wife in anger and it had not always been easy. There had been many scenes and arguments in his past, not so violent but equally devastating to his state of mind. Two or three times before she had slapped him when his rebuttals were sound and her exasperation got the best of her. But this—

Was it because in earlier days his self-control was better and pride prevented any retaliation? Or was his forbearance due to the fact that never before had their contentions seemed so important?

Was it the things she had said about Nancy, the inferences made? The thoughts of his son and the deep-seated resentment of this new request for custody?

His steps slowed as reason returned and the shakiness disappeared. There were no conclusive answers to his questions and presently hope came again. What had happened was over. He was ashamed and he would apologize. Frieda might not forget, but the fact that she had come to discuss divorce indicated that she was interested. There could be personal reasons, quite aside from Ricky, where none had existed before. If so, a compromise was possible.

Suppose he agreed to custody during vacations, holding out for one month in the summer. That would be better than nothing. Ricky would be thirteen in another couple of months. In three years he would be sixteen, nearly a man, and by then he would have some choice as to where, and with whom, he spent his vacations. Such thoughts were mildly cheering and he stopped at the side of the road, seeing the string of moving lights in the distance and realizing this must be the parkway.

Then he thought of Nancy and the instructions he had given her.

Wheeling, he started back, legs stretching. He had no idea how long he had been walking, but he had an idea about how far he had come. Hurrying now in the still night air, he could feel the perspiration come and his shirt was damp beneath his belt. Rounding a curve a car coming toward him swung wide and he stepped from the macadam. Another car not far behind gave him more room, and when he glanced over his shoulder after it had passed he thought it looked familiar.

It was moving too fast for him to read the license plate and he had the vague impression that a man was driving. But it was a convertible like his wife's. The general color scheme was similar, too, and as he plowed ahead, he hoped it was Frieda's. For there was no telling what she might do when she was angry, and although he had told Nancy not to stop if she saw Frieda's car, he did not want to encounter his wife again so soon.

He was panting slightly as he made the final turn into the straight stretch that led past his house. Ashley's place was still dark and a minute later he could tell that the convertible was gone. There was only his small sedan in the driveway as he cut across the lawn to the front door.

As he turned the knob he hesitated, to glance back at his car to make sure Nancy was not in it and then he went inside and through the little entryway. At first glance he thought the room was empty and started to call out; then, his gaze lowered, he saw the crumpled figure on the floor in front of the divan.

The next long seconds had no place in Rick Sheridan's memory then or later. What he did was automatic and without conscious thought because the conflict in his mind was too great.

In that first instant, as the shock hit him, he froze in his tracks, his body immobile and cold all over. He did not remember that he had left Frieda on the floor screaming at him; all he knew was that his car was outside, that the convertible was gone, that the woman on the floor had a white suit and blond hair.

There was no doubt in his mind. The first impression told him with a horrible certainty that Nancy must have come in while Frieda was still here and that Frieda, already gripped in a fit of fury and frustration, had killed her.

He wanted to cry out and his throat stayed closed. He put out a hand to steady himself. He pushed with that hand, forcing himself to move and, weak-kneed, he kept moving.

"Nancy!" he cried, his voice a ragged whisper. "Nancy."

Then, somehow, he was on his knees, the wonderment growing in him that the white suit he had seen from the doorway was in reality not a suit but a dress. The hair was blond but not as long as Nancy's. The face, in profile, was too thin.

Only then did he realize his mistake and know beyond all doubt that this was Frieda, and now, as some odd relief mixed with his horror, he saw the bruise on the throat, the scarf that had been cruelly twisted to leave a thin blue line in the skin.

The eyelids were closed and still. The distorted face had a bluish tinge beneath the tan, and the painted mouth was open. The straw handbag was open beside one outstretched hand, its contents spilled. It was when his glance moved on that the shadow of some movement caught the corner of his eye, and now, swiveling on one knee, he saw Nancy standing in the doorway to the inner hall, her eyes wide, her palms pressed hard against the sides of her taut white face.

3

FOR the next few agonizing seconds there was no sound in the room and neither of them moved. Out on the highway a car raced past and the sound of a girl's laughter drifted through the open door and served to break the spell that death had woven. Rick found he was holding his breath and let it out. He swallowd to loosen his throat.

"Nancy," he said huskily. "My God, Nancy!"

He pushed up from the floor and his knees were stiff. "Nancy," he said again, his voice quiet now, and with that she uttered a small cry and ran to him and flung her arms about him and held on hard.

"Oh, Rick," she wailed. "I was so frightened."

He could feel her tremble against him, hear the muffled sobs as she buried her face in his shoulder and reaction shook her. For a little while longer he did not know what to do or what to say. His glance came to the straw bag and he found himself checking the contents—the lipstick and keys and tissues; the cigarette case and gold lighter; the compact which had been jarred open to spill traces of powder on the rug.

Finally he took a breath and put his hands on her shoulders. He pushed gently and when she lifted her face he saw the dark lashes were matted and the green eyes wet. Still holding her shoulders he pushed her still farther from him and steadied his voice with an effort.

"What happened?"

"I—don't know, Rick. There wasn't any car outside and I thought—"

She swallowed and tried again.

"She was like that when I came in. I didn't know what happened. I didn't touch her but I saw her face. . . . Her face, Rick," she said, her voice breaking again. "All twisted and blue and—"

"All right." He made his voice sharp to blot out such memories and make her concentrate. "I know how you

22

must have felt, but right now we've got to think. Come here."

He led her to the nearest chair and pushed her gently back into it. He stepped over to the table and poured some brandy into the clean glass. He told her to take a swallow and waited until she had obeyed.

"Now," he said. "Think, darling. How long were you here?"

"Not more than a few minutes."

"How many? Four, five?"

"About that."

"Which way did you come from, the Sound side?"

"The other way."

"You didn't see anyone near here or any car?" He watched her shake her head, seeing the color coming back into her cheeks and aware from her frown that she was trying to think. "So you came in and found her just like that. You didn't touch her. Was there anything else—"

He stopped as a peculiar look came into her eyes. "Maybe I just imagined it," she said slowly. "But I was standing there looking down at Frieda and not knowing what had happened or why and I thought I heard something."

He waited, some new tension intermingling with his thoughts. "Like what?" he said.

"Like—well, it might have been a door closing. . . . Please, Rick, I'm not even sure I heard it. I could have imagined it; I could have imagined almost anything the way I felt."

"But you thought it was a door. Then what?"

"It sounded as if it came from somewhere out back and I started to look. I don't know what made me. If I had stopped to think, if I'd had any sense, I would have screamed and run out the front door."

Rick swore under his breath, not knowing whether all this was imagination or not but understanding that she had done a very foolish thing. In spite of himself his mind raced on to conjure up the frightening picture of what might have happened, and the question he asked had but one answer.

"You didn't see anything? Or hear anything more?"

"I went down the hall to the back door. I didn't dare look into the bedrooms. By then I was too busy telling myself it must have been my imagination. I was standing there by the hall doorway when I heard the front doorknob rattle and I didn't stop to think it might be you. I didn't know who it was. I just ran back into the bedroom."

Rick understood this much, for he too had jumped to conclusions about the body on the floor when he found the convertible gone and his sedan standing in its place. Now, aware that this was not the time for speculation, he took the glass from Nancy and asked if she wanted more brandy before he put the bottle away.

"No. . . . What're you going to do?"

"Call the police."

"Yes, I guess you have to." She stood up and took the bottle and glasses from him. "I can put that away. I'll rinse the glasses."

When he had been connected with the state police barracks he said what he had to say and then, as he put the telephone down, he realized that there was another call he had to make.

Frederick J. Brainard knew his daughter was coming here at nine. In the course of investigation the police would notify him. They would get his opinion of Rick Sheridan, would hear of a relationship that had been unfailingly unpleasant, would know why he wanted a divorce. Better then to tell him the shocking news by telephone and let him come tonight.

He had to look up the number and when he had his connection he had to identify himself before Brainard could be summoned. Even then Rick could feel the hostility in the blunt voice.

There is no easy way to break such news, no kind words to lessen the shock. Rick did as best he could, speaking hesitantly, using the words that came to him and hearing the spoken questions and reactions that were first unbelieving, then suspicious, and finally crushed.

"But strangled," Brainard said when he could accept the fact that his daughter was dead. "How could this happen? Who did it?"

"I don't know," Rick said. "It happened while I was out of the house. When I came back I found her on the floor. I've already called the police." He paused and the silence came to be broken by a single word that had a savage inflection.

"No!"

"What?"

"It didn't just happen. No one would just walk into a

house and do a thing like that. A man would have to have a reason and you had a reason, a good one. I know why she went there. She expected you'd fight with her—"

"Mr. Brainard!"

"I'll make no accusation until I have the facts, but I'm warning you now that I'll find out who did this if it takes every dollar I have. Remember that, Rick. If you happen to be the one, God help you!"

Rick heard the receiver crash down at the other end of the wire. He put the telephone gently in its cradle and wiped the perspiration from his brow. When he turned he found Nancy watching him with anxious eyes. She asked whom he was talking to and he told her. He did not add that Brainard already thought that he, Rick, had killed Brainard's daughter.

A state police cruiser was first on the scene, its occupant a burly, uniformed officer who listened briefly, looked long enough to make sure Frieda was dead, and then asked for the telephone. Another car came presently with two more uniformed men and after that Rick began to lose track of the others who came in civilian clothes.

He and Nancy were allowed to wait in the studio while the medical examiner performed his duties and the technical men went through their practiced routine. The captain of the western division came to question them briefly, but in the end the duties of investigation fell upon two men: a lieutenant from the Special Service branch of the state police, and the county detective representing the state's attorney's office.

The lieutenant's name was Legett, a tall, spare man of forty or so with a rectangular face and alert dark eyes. He wore beige tropical slacks and a lightweight sport jacket and no hat, so that there was only the quiet persistence of his manner and prying gaze to suggest to the uninitiated that he might be an officer of the law specializing in homicide. County Detective Manning was a rotund man of indeterminate age, who wore a gray business suit and metal-rimmed glasses. When they were ready for more detailed information they came into the studio, which was an extension of the living room.

"You were the one who found her, Miss Heath?" they said.

"Yes."

"We'd like to get your story," Legett said and nodded

toward the open doorway. "We can use another room."

Nancy stood up. Her face was composed now and as she straightened her shoulders and pulled down the jacket of her suit she glanced at Rick. He gave her a nod of encouragement and the best smile he could; then watched proudly as she marched from the room with her chin up.

When he had a cigarette going he looked slowly about the paneled room. He considered the two illustrations he had done for True-Fruit, which stood propped against the wall on the old trestle table, wondering if he would be able to deliver them to Ted Banks in the morning. Both were boy-girl jobs, one showing the edge of a tennis court and the other at dockside with the boy and girl in bathing suits looking down at a sailboat which had been moored there.

One of the advantages of having an agent nowadays was the equipment and studio room such agents provided. Ted Banks and his partner had a whole floor in a mid-town building, and in addition to the private cubbies for each artist who wanted one, there was a well-equipped photographic studio. With model prices the way they were, most artists posed their people the way they wanted them and got their photographs in an hour or so, using the prints to work from later on. In Rick's case he did most of his roughs at the studio and his finished art here in the country at this time of year.

He considered the portrait of Elinor Farrell and decided he had no worries in that direction since it was practically finished. He looked at the homemade racks in the corner where his unframed but completed work was stacked. Free-lance work, mostly oils, with a few in gouache and tempera, of various sizes and subjects, some fairly recent but most of them old.

A few were experiments done between the big war and Korea, but the majority had been done at Frieda's insistence after he had come back the second time. She had never had any objection to his being an artist but she had argued for serious art, and prestige; something, as she put it, she could be proud of. He was still working on salary for the advertising agency then and he had painted furiously in his spare time, knowing somehow that his work was not quite right but not certain why. His draftsmanship was excellent and he was a pretty fair colorist but his brushwork was not good enough. The one-man show that

Frieda arranged for him proved it, at least for the time being.

He had sold two pictures. When commissions were paid he barely made expenses, and the fact that she could support him while he perfected his techniques was an argument that had no appeal. He did three portraits for wealthy friends of hers and felt they were quite good, but he knew then that for him the so-called serious art must wait. It would be wonderful indeed to be another Eakins or Homer or Bellows or Hopper some day, but for the present he wanted to be a successful illustrator and that meant the advertising field.

It seemed now that he had been right. He had sold his work right from the start, small things in black and white first, taking what he could get and doing the best he could with it. He was not yet getting top prices and the demand for his color work was spotty, but he was getting there—

He snapped his thoughts in place at the sound of some commotion in the other room and when he glanced through the doorway he caught a glimpse of Frederick Brainard. He could hear his voice mingling with others but the words remained indistinct. He knew he would eventually have to face his father-in-law and the prospect was discouraging because Brainard had blamed him for the original elopement, and his dislike for Rick had been consistent over the years. He knew, too, that the man loved his daughter despite the fact that they were usually at odds over some matter. Now, because he had no choice, Rick could only wait and it took longer than he thought. It was nearly a half hour later that Brainard came through the doorway with Lieutenant Legett at his side and advanced two steps before he stopped.

Rick stood up, not knowing what to expect, and in the silent moment that they stood there with eyes locked, he remembered again that Frederick J. Brainard was a man of some importance in Fairfield County.

There were many more wealthy but few who had taken more interest in public affairs and local politics, possibly because Brainard was not a commuter. As president of the Brainard Tool Company, which had been founded by his grandfather, he ruled a modest but prosperous business with its principal plant near Greenwich, and his water-front estate was not far away.

A well-setup and vigorous man in his late fifties, he had thick gray hair, a stubborn, muscular jaw, and an outdoor look that was genuine and came from golf and sailing. Generally respected for his integrity, he was to many a domineering man, determined to win all battles whether business or personal and impatient with failure. His character was deficient in some things, chiefly a sense of humor, and to Rick there had always been a lack of sympathy and the ability to see any side of an argument but his own. Now the face had a grayish tinge and his voice was thick and unsteady.

"I've told the detectives about you and Frieda," he said. "And the divorce and why she came here tonight. I also told them about her inheritance."

He hesitated and Rick waited, understanding how hard the man had been hit, seeing the signs of grief that could not be hidden, and finding no words that could express his sympathy. That Brainard might accuse him surprised him not at all and, at the moment, he did not even resent the words that followed.

"I've told them that, in my opinion, you're the only man who had a possible motive to do such a thing." He paused again, mouth working. When he started to move forward, Legett touched his arm and he stopped.

"Remember what I told you over the phone," he said, his voice breaking with emotion. "If you did it, so help me, I'll see that you pay if it's the last thing I do."

He stopped abruptly, shoulders sagging. He let Legett turn him toward the door. A moment later he was gone and Rick suddenly felt tired and old and despondent. He crushed out his cigarette, and because he could no longer stand still, he began to pace the room, head down and eyes brooding. He was still at it when he heard a new voice in the other room. By the time he could turn, Tom Ashley was walking toward him, Legett trailing.

"Jesus, Rick!" Ashley shook hands hard. "I just found out about Frieda. I don't know what to say. I still can't believe it." He gave Rick's hand another hard squeeze and let go. "Is there anything I can do? If there's anything at all—"

"Thanks, Tom. There isn't anything anyone can do right now."

"Well, do you—" He broke off to turn on Legett. "Do you guys have any idea—"

"Not yet, Mr. Ashley." Legett's eyes had been busy and now his tone was casual. "You're Mr. Sheridan's next door neighbor?"

"That's right. The little white house. I drove up and saw all the cars and the lights, so I came over."

"You weren't home this evening."

"No."

"Mind telling us where you were?"

"Hell, no. I went out to eat around seven thirty or a quarter of eight," he said, and named a restaurant.

"How long were you there?"

"I don't know. I had a couple of drinks. Maybe an hour and a quarter or so."

"That would make it around nine or a little before." Legett glanced at his strap watch. "It's now ten forty."

"Well?"

"Where did you go after you left the restaurant?"

"I drove out along the shore and parked."

"Alone?"

Until then Ashley's replies had been quick and matter of fact. Now he hesitated, a small frown warping his brows and his eyes narrowing. For the first time he seemed to sense that the questions were not idle ones, that Legett was investigating a murder and still looking for suspects. His shoulders straightened slightly and they were thick shoulders, for Ashley was a strongly built man, hard-necked and bulky in his slacks and sport shirt.

"Yes, Lieutenant," he said, "and if that sounds a little fishy to you I'll try to explain it. I'm a writer. I spend ninety per cent of my time not writing but thinking. To think, I have to be alone and I like it quiet if possible. I can show you where I parked and the cigarette I chucked out the window if that'll be of any help."

The pointed irony of such an explicit explanation was not lost on Legett, but he gave no sign that it bothered him. He lean face remained impassive and his voice was unchanged.

"You know Mrs. Sheridan?"

"Certainly. She published my first two books."

"How many have you written?"

"Three."

"Who published the third?"

"Nobody—yet." For an instant Ashley's gaze wavered. "I just finished it. I haven't signed a contract with anybody."

"Did you know she was coming here tonight?"

"No," Ashley said and then his eyes flickered to Rick and he seemed to realize that such a statement might trap him. "What I mean is, Rick told me over the phone this afternoon that she was coming but I didn't know when."

Legett had a few more routine questions which Ashley answered, but by that time Rick was no longer listening; instead his mind had moved backward as he recalled that Ashley had once been very friendly with Frieda.

In a way Ashley was responsible for his building in that neighborhood. For he had met the writer at a party in Wilton over a year ago when Ashley was finishing his second book. Both had been stags at the party and they'd had quite a bit to drink and they wound up late at Ashley's house where Rick had spent the night.

He had already been thinking of building a house and the following day Ashley introduced him to a real estate man and the three of them looked for likely locations. In the end Rick settled for the adjoining two acres, and as time went on they had become good friends.

Ashley's first book had been a critical success but had not earned much in the way of royalties. Frieda's firm had published it and Rick knew that she had worked hard in helping Ashley with the second one, which turned out to be a resounding hit. Ashley knew about the separation and he had made sure of Rick's attitude before admitting that he was seeing a lot of Frieda during the time he was working on the book. In more recent months there had been no mention of Frieda, and Rick had the impression that the affair, if there had been one, had petered out. He did know that Ashley was now engaged to a girl in Westport whose family was socially prominent. He had met the girl—she was only twenty-two—and had found her engaging, attractive, and apparently entirely sold on Ashley. . . .

"All right, Mr. Ashley," Legett was saying by way of dismissal. "We'll be in touch with you. Thanks for your help."

"Sure." Ashley nodded to Rick. "Don't forget, chum. Anything you want, just yell."

When Legett came back he had the county detective with him and this time they shut the door and asked Rick to sit down. Manning took a small notebook out of his pocket and gave it his attention while Legett started the ball rolling.

"Miss Heath has told her story," he said, "and now we'd like to hear yours. Take it from the time you got out of the car here and tell it in your own words."

Rick did the best he could and it did not take long. When he finished, Manning cleared his throat.

"How long have you wanted this divorce?" he asked in flat, impersonal tones.

"I began to think about it a couple of months ago."

"Because you wanted to marry Miss Heath."

"Right."

"What was your wife's reaction?"

"Negative. She said she'd think about it, and why did I want it. You know—things like that."

"When did you talk about it again?"

"Last week."

"What did she say that time?"

"She said she liked the arrangement we had."

"She must have said more than that."

"She said a lot more than that," Rick said as he recalled the rather stormy scene and Frieda's announcement that if he tried to get a divorce she would probably fight it. "But what it amounted to was that she had no intention of making it easy for me to marry Miss Heath."

"She wasn't in love with you—your wife, I mean?"

"Not for years."

"The feeling was mutual?"

"It was."

"Then why do you think she refused to co-operate. Was it a question of money?"

"No. I think she just wanted to be difficult."

"Were you surprised when she phoned this afternoon and said she was ready to talk? Have you any idea what changed her mind?"

Rick thought about this before he replied. He had no way of knowing if something had happened in Frieda's personal life that made her find a divorce desirable, or whether her father had instigated the offer. For Brainard saw in Ricky the son he had never had; he would have liked nothing better than to bring the boy up as he saw fit and without interference from Rick.

"No," he said. "I don't know why she changed her mind."

"Did you reach an agreement tonight?"

"No."

"Why not?"

"She wanted full custody of my son and I wouldn't go for it."

Manning cleared his throat again and exchanged glances with Legett. "You said before that you had an argument and you walked out on your wife. Why? Because you were afraid you might kill her?"

The question was so close to the truth it put Rick on the defensive and his reply was both resentful and irritated.

"Are you married, Manning?"

"We're talking about you, Mr. Sheridan."

"Okay. We had an argument. We wound up shouting and getting nowhere and I walked out because I was sore. I've done it before and so have a million other guys because when you get into that kind of argument with your wife you can't win."

"There was a bruise on one cheek," Legett said. "Know anything about that?"

"No," Rick said, lying because he was afraid of the truth.

"You walked out," Manning said. "Her car was there. You kept walking." He glanced at his notebook. "You don't know how long you were gone but when you got back your wife's car was gone and you found Miss Heath with your wife's body."

"Not with the body. She was in another room."

"Miss Heath said she got here about a quarter of ten and you came four or five minutes later," Legett said. "What do you think happened to that convertible."

"I don't know."

"Do you want to guess?"

"She could have picked someone up after she left her father's place—"

"You mean a hitchhiker?" Manning asked.

"No. Someone she had a date with. He could have been sitting in the car waiting for her—I didn't even look at it—and if there was anyone in the car he could have killed her and then driven it off."

"Where?"

"How do I know? Maybe to the station."

"We're a little partial to motive in cases like this," Manning said. "And I wouldn't kid you. You've got a beaut. Maybe you've read about such things in the papers. A guy nuts about some girl and the wife holding out on the divorce. Sometimes the wife gets killed."

Rick made no answer but he knew with discouraging certainty that it had happened before; could even have happened tonight if he had not run away.

"There's another motive, too," Legett said. "Your father-in-law says your wife inherited a trust fund from her mother. About two hundred thousand at the time. Worth about four hundred thousand now. Do you know what happens to that money?"

Rick had forgotten about the trust fund but he knew the terms well enough. The income from the fund was to be Frieda's until she was forty, at which time she got control of the principal. Now that she was dead the money would be held in trust for Ricky to be his when he was twenty-one.

"I know what happens," he said, "but what about it? That money will never be mine."

"Suppose the boy dies, too?"

Rick started out of the chair, his face stiff and pale at the cheekbones, his eyes hard as they fixed on Manning's round bespectacled features.

Legett moved in front of him, his tone placating.

"Easy, Mr. Sheridan. Right now we're considering all possibilities."

The county detective seemed not to have moved a muscle. He sat where he was, his gaze reflective. Under its spell Rick calmed down and measured his words.

"I didn't kill my wife," he said. "I happen to love my son very dearly."

"Mr. Brainard tells us," Manning continued as though he had not heard, "that his daughter got about fifteen thousand a year from that trust before taxes. That income is yours to do with as you please until the boy's of age. In my book that's a motive."

He heaved out of the chair and put his notebook away. After a glance at Legett he said: "Let's go down and get some of this on paper, Mr. Sheridan."

"What about Nancy Heath?"

"She'll have to come, too."

"Why? She told you—"

"She's a witness. She'll have to sign a statement. There's a policewoman with her now."

"But—she lives in New York. How long will she have to stay?"

"I don't know. But when she's finished, if she wants transportation to New York, we can provide it."

4

RICK SHERIDAN never remembered too many details of the night he spent in the state police barracks. He told his story twice more and answered countless questions before a statement was typed and offered for his signature, and between such sessions there were times when he was left alone in the little office for considerable periods. Once a uniformed officer brought him a sandwich and coffee and later someone got him cigarettes from the machine in the hall. The sky was getting light in the east when they told him he could go, and as he passed the office at the front of the building Nancy called to him.

The furniture indicated that this was probably the office of the commanding officer but there was no one behind the desk at this hour, only Nancy and an attractive, dark-haired policewoman. They were having coffee and sitting close together in friendly fashion, and for a moment Rick just looked at them in open-eyed amazement.

"Nancy," he said. "Have you been here all this time? I thought you were home hours ago." He looked at the policewoman and continued indignantly. "What's the idea of holding her here all night?"

"They didn't, Rick."

"She wanted to wait," the policewoman said. "Would you like some coffee?"

Such cheerful hospitality took the edge from his concern and he mumbled his thanks as he refused. Nancy put her cup aside and stood up. "Thanks awfully, Alice," she said and shook hands with the woman as though they were good friends; then she was walking out the door with Rick, her arm locked with his.

"She's really very nice," she said.

"Who?" said Rick, his thoughts on more serious matters.

"Alice. She told me about her work. Some of it sounds fascinating."

34

He gave her arm a shake. "Look, baby," he said, having no time for her impressions of Alice, "when did you finish? When did they say you could go?"

"About two or a little after. They asked a million questions, mostly the same ones over and over."

"Did they offer to take you home?"

"Oh, yes. But I told them I'd rather wait for you."

Rick shook his head. He sighed and let his breath out. To himself he said, *What a girl.* Aloud he said: "How did you know they were going to let me go at all?"

"I didn't. They told me they didn't know about that but I thought if they *did* let you out in time I'd rather ride to town with you. If they didn't—well, someone has to deliver that True-Fruit art to Ted Banks this morning, and I could do it for you."

They were at his car by then, and when he had opened the door he stopped to take her hands in his and smile down at her. When he saw the green eyes soften and smile back at him he sighed again.

"You're wonderful," he said. "I love you. . . . Get in. How about a shower and some breakfast?"

"I'd love it."

In the light of day the living room showed obvious signs of the official invasion. Traces of dusting powder smudged the woodwork here and there, the ashtrays were filled to overflowing, and one wastebasket held a half dozen used flashbulbs. When Nancy started to straighten up Rick stopped her, saying he would call Mrs. Furman, the cleaning woman who came regularly three mornings a week.

"You can take your bath first if you still want it. I'll get the coffee started and squeeze some oranges."

During the night the breeze had shifted to the easterly quadrant, cooling itself before moving inland, and it was bright and pleasant at five minutes of eight as Rick drove up the ramp to the parkway. Little had been said since they left the house and presently Nancy voiced a thought that had been bothering Rick for some time.

"What are you going to do about Ricky?"

He could make no immediate answer to the question but he could see in fancy the camp buildings in the pine grove at the edge of the Adirondack lake. It was not the de luxe sort of camp that is advertised in some of the better magazines but it had been highly recommended by two of Rick's friends, and he had been impressed by the man who had directed the camp for more than twenty years and by the number of college boy counselors who worked there each summer.

The values that Rick wanted his son to know were taught here in a simple and direct way and each camper had work to do. His allowance was limited and parental visits were discouraged except on Sundays; punishment, when necessary, took the form of additional chores and loss of privileges. His son had thrived on such a regime and Rick remembered the last Sunday that he had driven up there with Nancy, who had come bearing a gift.

When he had thanked her, Ricky had eyed the candy box curiously and then, glancing up, had asked if he could open it now.

"Of course," Nancy said, and they watched him loosen the ribbon and lift the lid to find three layers of brownies neatly fitted inside.

"Boy," he said joyously. "Brownies. Homemade, too."

"Sure they're homemade," Rick said.

Then, as though aware of his obligations, Ricky extended the box. "Will you have one, Nancy?" he said, remembering that she had asked him to call her by her first name.

Nancy said no, that they were for him, and Rick, very proud now but finding a small lump in his throat, rumpled his son's blond hair.

"Just be sure you share them with your tentmates."

"Oh, sure, Dad," the boy had said. "All the guys do."

Rick's thoughts jerked back to his problem when he heard Nancy's voice. "I'm sorry," he said. "I guess I wasn't listening."

"I—I was wondering if you'd like me to tell him. I could get the day off and drive up there—"

"No," Rick said. "I want to talk to him but he may be off somewhere. They're always having projects of some kind up there." He drove another silent mile and said: "I think I'll talk to Pop Wayne, the camp director, first. He understands a boy's mind better than I do and Ricky thinks he's the greatest guy in the world."

"Next to you."

"And I can see what Pop says and then fix it so I can call back again and talk to Ricky." He hesitated, his thoughts depressed and uncertain. "Right now I don't know what I want to say. I don't know when the funeral will be or what Mr. Brainard wants to do or whether I should tell Ricky to come or tell him to stay."

"Couldn't you—well, sort of leave it up to Ricky? He's nearly thirteen."

"Maybe you're right."

"You can probably sense how he feels about it when you talk to him. It might be kinder to let him remember his mother the way he last saw her but I don't think I'd be insistent no matter what he decides."

They fell silent after that and it was not until they were on the outskirts of the city that he spoke of the other matter which could no longer be ignored.

"I've got to have help, Nancy."

"About Ricky?"

"About me. I don't know what's going to happen. Unless the police find out who killed Frieda I may have to stand trial for murder."

"I don't believe it. How can—"

"And even if I don't," he said, ignoring the outburst, "I'll always be under suspicion. Suppose they don't try me? Suppose they don't try anybody? The fact is, somebody *did* kill her. If this thing isn't cleared up Brainard is going to keep on thinking I did it and got away with it. I certainly had good motives. People are going to keep wondering. How can Ricky be sure when he grows up? How would you like to be the wife of a guy whose first wife died in an unsolved murder?"

"But I know you didn't do it."

She hesitated, and a sidwise glance told him that the thought had frightened her.

"Your friends will know you couldn't have done it," she said, but her argument was more stubborn than convincing.

"We'll go to parties and even if people aren't wondering they'll remember what happened. We'll never know for sure what they're thinking and it'll always be there beneath the surface. And that'll be the best that can happen. I may even be in jail tomorrow and—"

"Please, Rick," she cried. "Don't talk like that."

"But it's true." He rapped the wheel with the heel of his hand. "So long as the police figure me as the prime suspect they're bound to try to clinch the case. Let's not kid about it. I've got to get something working on my side while I've still got time."

She leaned back in the seat, shoulders slumping and her

hands limp in her lap. After a while she said:

"Do you know anyone you can talk to?"

"I'll call Neil Tyler, my lawyer, first and see what he says. I might as well get him prepared. Maybe he can recommend a good private investigator."

"All right," she said quietly. "And I can get time off from my job if there's any way I can help."

He put his hand on her knee and squeezed gently. "That's better," he said, and with the words, felt a little better himself.

5

THE SIGN on the door said: THE CROMBIE AGENCY and gave no clue as to the type of business pursued inside. It was on the fourth floor of a nondescript office building on Seventh Avenue in the forties, and when Rick Sheridan walked in he found himself in a small, squarish room furnished with a settee, four chairs, and a low table cluttered with dog-eared magazines. One wall had a glass window with a semi-circular opening, beyond which a bright-eyed brunette sat at a switchboard. When Rick gave his name she smiled at him and pressed a button which clicked the latch of a door next to the window.

"Yes, Mr. Sheridan," she said. "Mr. Crombie's expecting you. Straight down to the corner office."

Once inside, Rick saw that the open space beyond the switchboard was occupied by two girls who were working at their desks. On the right he passed three tiny, glass-partitioned cubbyholes, and that brought him to the office at the end which was not a great deal larger.

A desk had been moved diagonally across one corner. Seated behind it was a man of considerable bulk who wore cord trousers—the jacket was draped over a hanger and topped by a Panama hat—and a white shirt. He looked to be about fifty, his gray eyes were bright and keen behind the drooping lids, and in spite of his weight and the noticeable paunch he came easily to his feet.

"I'm Rick Sheridan," Rick said. "I think Neil Tyler called you."

Crombie offered a big hand that looked fat but proved to be surprisingly hard. "Sam Crombie," he said. "Sit down, Mr. Sheridan."

Rick took the only other chair and Crombie let himself down in a desk chair which creaked with his weight. He tipped back and put his hands behind his neck, locking his fingers there. When he continued, his voice carried overtones of some hoarseness that seemed chronic but the cadence was low pitched, with a minimum of inflection.

"Mr. Tyler told me a little about what happened to you last night," he said, "and you have my sympathy. I understand you and your wife weren't too friendly but murder is always a shocking business even when it happens to strangers. I'm not sure what you have in mind, or if I can be of any help or not, but if you want to tell me about it I'll be better able to make an intelligent comment."

He swiveled his chair as Rick began to talk, hooking one foot on a drawer pull and his gaze fastened on the lone window which gave him a view of the walls of two near-by buildings. He made no interruption, nor did he shift his glance, until Rick had finished his account. After a few seconds of silent inaction, he swung the chair back and brought his gaze to focus.

"What you want from me is help in clearing yourself of suspicion?"

"Yes."

"I can see why. But I think I should tell you now that we seldom get involved in a murder case. Our work is usually pretty routine—checking up on people for any number of reasons, security work, things like that. The police have the manpower, equipment, and specialists to investigate a murder; we haven't."

"Oh," said Rick, his disappointment showing as his hopes faded. "Then you'd rather not handle it for me."

"I didn't say that. I just wanted you to get straight what we can do and what we can't. In this case there's one way we might help. You say you didn't kill her, so someone else did. With the outline you've given me it looks as if it was a murder that depended on circumstances rather than anything that had been planned. It apparently was done in a fit of anger—that's usually the case when a woman is strangled—by a man who knew your wife was going to be there at that time. It's possible, of course, that someone just happened to stop in at that moment after you'd gone. From what you say she was in a pretty nasty mood and—well, it could happen."

He hesitated, his gray eyes busy with thought. "What I'm getting at is that whoever killed her—I'm ruling out a prowler now—had a damn good motive, at least to him. The desire to kill, maybe even the necessity to kill, must have been in his mind, and when the opportunity came he took it. Why?" he said, and answered himself. "Because he hated her or because he was afraid of her and knew she was a threat to his security or future. . . . Maybe I'm not putting this very well but do you get what I mean?"

"I know exactly what you mean," Rick said, because the picture Crombie offered helped to clarify his own thoughts.

"So we can do this: we can check into your wife's personal life the last couple of years. We can find out who her friends are, who she's been going out with and, unless she's been living like a nun, who she might have been intimate with. It might help some if you'd tell me more about her, and yourself for that matter. What's her background? How long have you been married?"

Rick told him how he had met Frieda and spoke of the elopement. He said they were kids at the time but he had already decided to drop out of college at the end of his junior year and go to Officers' Candidate School.

"Had you met her father before you eloped?"

"Sure," Rick said. "She had me out to the house for a week end. When the old boy found out I had barely enough money to finish school he lost interest in me. When he learned I wanted to be an artist he went to work on Frieda."

"Who thought up the elopement?"

"Well—we wanted to get married and there wasn't any other way. I think one reason Frieda wanted to elope was to get away from her father. Her mother died when she was ten and her father always wanted a son, and he's one of those guys who have to boss every operation they're involved in. He dominated Frieda when he could, and made her decisions, and he forgot that there were a lot of his qualities in her. She'd fight him—I guess it got to be a complex—but when she was young she still had to knuckle under. With me I guess she figured she would be herself for a change. Even later when she'd go back for the summer or a week end she went on her own terms, and the funny thing is, the older she got the more bossy she got."

"Like her old man."

Rick nodded, offered a cigarette, which was refused, and lit his own. "She wanted to be a big shot," he said. "She wanted to be important and be seen with what she thought was the right people. That's why she wheedled fifty thousand from the executors of her mother's estate and started this book publishing firm with another man."

"Go back aways," Crombie said in his flat hoarse voice. "Did you always want to be an artist?"

"Not when I was a kid. But I could always draw. I did cartoons for the high-school paper and kept it up in college for the humorous magazine. I began taking all the art courses I could and when I was in Germany I did some posters and filled two or three notebooks with sketches. The baby was born while I was over there and I arranged to get discharged in Paris, figuring on having Frieda and the boy come over so I could study a while longer on the G.I. bill."

He paused, slouching in his chair as his thoughts embraced well-remembered details and recalling again his disappointment when Frieda had refused to come. For he had already signed up for certain courses, and had found a small apartment, all of which had to be canceled so he could take the next boat home.

"She was living with her father then and I didn't even have a job, so I couldn't argue. But I looked up some college friends and got a start with Byron & Cowles—that's one of the better advertising agencies—doing layouts and roughs for dummies and direct-mail pieces."

He digressed to speak of Frieda's trust fund and said that by then she had begun to get the income from it.

"She also had a nurse for the baby, and a maid. It was her money and I couldn't very well tell her how to spend it," he said. "So we had a fine apartment, with me making seventy-five bucks a week and going to art school three nights a week. She had about a year of chasing around with her café friends, staying up most of the night and sleeping all morning."

"But you still got along," Crombie said. "You were still sleeping together."

"Oh, sure," Rick said. "I was busy, and so was she in her way. I was crazy about the boy and it didn't matter then whether she was too busy to give him any time. Then she got bored and decided she wanted to work. She got a job as a reader with a publishing house and we didn't do too badly together until Korea came along and the army decided I was indispensable. I was away nearly a year and a half and when I got back things were different."

"In what way?"

"In every way. She was thinner and edgy and businesslike and efficient. The warmth I remembered was gone. She was just starting this publishing house with a guy named

Eastman who had been a sales manager for another firm. We had a bigger apartment and Ricky was in day school and she said it was time we had our own rooms. I don't mean there was no more sex but it only happened once in a while, maybe when we'd been out together and had a few drinks and she forgot her business ambitions long enough to remember that she was still a woman.

"By that time," he said, "I'd started to free-lance and I was working like a dog because my rates were low and I had to scratch and take what my agent lined up for me. As a matter of fact I was lucky to get a good agent as soon as I did." He put his cigarette out and tipped his hand in an empty gesture.

"That's about it. Two years ago we just decided what we had was no good for either of us. She didn't have any marriage plans and neither did I, so we decided a separation would be the best thing."

"Umm." Crombie picked up a pad and a pencil, his chair creaking as he let his weight come forward. "She sounds like a woman who'd want a man around just the same. If she wants to be a big shot like you say and likes to get around the right places she'd need someone, wouldn't she? A woman like that wouldn't want to go alone."

Rick cocked his head as his respect for the detective began to mount. Because Frieda did need men, but on her terms. She hated to be alone. She wanted company and attention quite aside from any physical need she may have felt, and Rick was no longer sure about this aspect of her character. He said as much to Crombie and the detective came directly to the point.

"Do you think she was a nymph?"

Rick considered the question and shook his head. "No."

"Promiscuous?"

"No. I think she had too much pride and integrity for that sort of thing. I think—" He paused to ask himself exactly what he did think. He tried to compare the fun-loving and passionate girl he had married with the woman he had talked with last night. "I think, if she liked a man real well, she might fall for him on a temporary basis. She might have an affair if she was sure of the man and it suited her."

"What I'm trying to do," Crombie said, "is find out if there's anyone who might have had an affair with her, or any reason to hate her. You got any ideas who she might have played around with?"

With his thoughts channeled into the proper perspective, Rick remembered Tom Ashley. Ashley had seen a lot of Frieda at one period; he had admitted this to Rick at the time and asked if he minded. He wondered now if the relationship had been limited to the work they had done on his books. He spoke of this now and Crombie nodded without looking up.

He was busy with his pad and pencil and Rick thought he was making notes until he gave a closer look and realized the man was doodling. Now, when the detective glanced up and found Rick watching him, he grinned crookedly.

"A habit," he said. "Seems to help me think. . . . Who else besides this Ashley?"

Rick mentioned Austin Farrell but admitted that here his knowledge was mostly hearsay. He had heard that Austin and Frieda had been together often in various night clubs and eating places, but that was the extent of his information.

"What's he do?" Crombie asked.

"Runs a small literary agency but he's got a rich wife." Rick went on to speak of the accident which had invalided Elinor Farrell permanently, and having seen them together on occasion he added that Farrell seemed very devoted to his wife, at least when he was with her.

"Does he impress you as the type your wife might go for?"

Recalling Farrell's manners, good looks, and impeccable grooming, Rick said: "Yes."

Crombie had gone back to his doodling. "Who else?"

"I don't know any other man except Clyde Eastman."

"Who's he?"

"Her partner in the publishing business."

"He might know quite a lot."

"I guess that's about all," Rick said and pushed back in his chair.

"Not quite all." Crombie glanced up, his gray gaze speculative. "You wanted a divorce. What about the girl you want it for?"

"Oh. . . . Her name's Nancy Heath," Rick said, and then he was telling how Nancy did layout and copy for a small advertising agency that specialized in publishing accounts.

The rest of it came easily as he told about meeting her one afternoon several months ago when he had stopped in Brainard & Eastman's to see Frieda, and Nancy had been there to get an okay on some copy. They had left together and it had been raining at the time and he had given her a lift in his taxi. A couple of weeks later she had called to ask if he would be interested in doing an illustration for a dust jacket wanted by another publisher. Working together on this had given him a chance to understand how attractive and desirable she was, how easy to talk to. They'd had drinks together when he delivered his work and that was all until another job renewed the association. This time the drinks carried over to dinner.

Without thinking too much about it he found himself wanting to see her with increasing frequency. He had driven her up to the camp to see Ricky and when he saw what a hit she made with his son it finally dawned on him that he was in love with her. He said nothing about this until they had gone to the camp a second time, and it was on the way back when they stopped for dinner that he knew for certain how she felt about him. Only then did it become important for him to have a divorce, to know that for them it was the only solution.

"Yeah," said Crombie, "and thanks for spelling it out. I don't want to sound like a marriage counselor but the more I can get from you about the background of this business the less waste motion we'll have later on. If your girl has been working with your wife's outfit she might know a few things that could help. . . . Okay."

He threw aside his pencil and leaned back again. His broad, hard jaw moved as he flexed his lips, and his eyes were thoughtful.

"Maybe we can help," he said, "but if time's important—and it looks like it is—it's not a one-man job and it won't be cheap."

"I don't care—"

"But you ought to know how it works. I've got three good men here with me and I can always get more. For them it costs thirty bucks a day, for eight hours. If they're working ten or twelve that goes down as two days; I mean that's what you're charged for. And, of course, always expenses."

"All right," Rick said. "But I want you on this."

"I come higher. I get double. Sixty bucks a day."

"Well, will you do it? Can you start now?"

"I'll have to re-arrange some things—" He paused and then nodded as his decision was made. "Yes. I don't see why not."

Rick gave a small sigh of relief when the answer came because it had suddenly become tremendously important that he have Sam Crombie's help. This talk, the opportunity to speak of things too long bottled up inside him, had done him a lot of good, having somehow a therapeutic effect that bolstered his courage and gave him new confidence. This, he knew, was not only a shrewd and experienced detective but one he could trust without reservation.

"Good," he said, and stood up, his problem solved until he glanced at his watch and saw that it was five minutes after twelve. That made him think of his son and the call he had made to the camp director from his lawyer's office. This was the time. Noon hour. Somehow, he was not sure just how, he must talk to the boy and hope he said the right things. When he told Crombie what he had to do the detective nodded and said to tell his operator what he wanted.

He pushed the telephone across the desk and started to stand up and Rick motioned him back. Somehow Crombie's presence seemed to bolster his resolve and lend the moral support that he so badly needed. He gave the operator the number and said to make the call person-to-person.

"I want to speak to Richard Sheridan."

He sat hunched in his chair, head down, holding the telephone loosely and feeling the moisture start to accumulate on his palm. But the call came through surprisingly quick and when he heard the small uncertain voice of his son he said:

"Ricky. . . . Did Pop Wayne tell you about your mother?"

"Yes. . . . Are you all right, Dad?"

The unexpectedness of the question jolted him and the concern in the boy's voice was so genuine that he felt a sudden weakness come over him.

"Me? Of course."

"But Pop said it happened at your house—"

"Yes, Ricky. But I wasn't there. She was alone."

"Oh." A long pause. "Do they think—was it a burglar, Dad?"

"It could have been. The police aren't sure."

Rick swallowed, his scalp prickling as the perspiration

began to come. What should he say? What could one say to a twelve-year-old boy when you didn't know how he felt about death or even how he felt about his mother?

"I don't know just what to tell you, Ricky. It happened. It happens every day to other people and this time it happened to us. We don't know how but we have to accept it, both of us. We have to take it. I wish I could be with you now but maybe it's better that you're up there with your friends."

There was no reply to this and he knew he must speak about the funeral. But here, too, he felt helpless and ineffective. Should he insist that the boy come or should he insist that he stay?

"I don't know when the funeral will be; probably not for two or three days. I'd like you to think about—whether you feel you want to come or stay in camp."

"I'll do whatever you say, Dad."

"Suppose you think about it before you decide, Son. When did you see your mother last?"

"I think it was in June. She had me come in town and we had lunch."

"Did you have a good time? Did you enjoy yourself?"

"Oh, sure."

"Then maybe you'd rather remember her as she was then. You know—how she looked and what she said. Maybe you'd like to think that she's just gone on a long trip and may never come back. . . . You think about it, Ricky."

He had to stop again. His throat seemed stuck and he had to clear it and he could feel the sting of tears in his eyes.

"You're a young man now and you'll have to start making up your own mind. . . . Will you do that, Ricky? Will you think about it? Or maybe you want to talk to Pop Wayne. I'll call you again when I know more about it and you can tell me then. . . . Okay?"

"Okay, Dad."

He waited, listening, and there was nothing more but the distant breaking of the connection. He put the telephone back, his fingers unsteady and his face wet. He swallowed again and reached for his handkerchief and when he glanced up Crombie's gaze was sympathetic. He had been obviously touched by what he had heard and the hoarseness of his voice was more pronounced.

"Yeah," he said. "A man doesn't know what to say at a time like that."

"I did the best I could," Rick said simply.

"You did all right." He pushed back his chair, his tone abruptly businesslike. "If you want to wait in the ante-room I'll be with you in a couple of minutes."

When Crombie appeared five minutes later he had his jacket on; the Panama hat rode on the center of his head.

"I've been thinking," he said, "that it might be a good idea to have a look at your wife's apartment—if you think we can get in."

Rick said the superintendent knew him and there should be no trouble and Crombie said: "But first let's have a talk with this partner of hers. He should be able to give us some angles that might be worth while."

6

THE OFFICES of Brainard & Eastman were on the seventh floor of a Forty-Sixth Street building close by Fifth Avenue. The receptionist recognized Rick at once and when he told her what he wanted she relayed his request.

"You can go right in, Mr. Sheridan," she said.

Rick led the way down the hall to a door at the end, knocked once and walked into a squarish, well-appointed office that had green wall-to-wall carpeting, an impressive-looking desk, a wall full of books, and an air-conditioning unit in one of the two windows. At one side of the desk a cellarette stood open. There was a whisky bottle and a thermos jug on top and a partly filled glass was in plain sight on the desk.

Clyde Eastman stood up as the door closed and shook hands. "Hello, Rick." He indicated a folded newspaper on a corner of the desk. "I didn't know a thing about it until I read the paper coming in on the train. What the hell can I say? I never thought things like that happened to people you knew. Why?" he demanded. "Do you know who did it yet?"

Rick said not yet and introduced Crombie, waiting until they had shaken hands before he added: "Mr. Crombie's a detective."

Eastman's pale-blue eyes opened wide. "A cop?"

"Private, Mr. Eastman," Crombie said.

Eastman turned his still wide-open gaze at Rick. "What do you need a detective for?"

"I'm in a jam," Rick said. "The police seem to think I might be the one that killed Frieda."

"They must be nuts."

Eastman picked up his glass, studied it morosely. When he had drained the drink he looked at Rick.

"I don't suppose you want a touch? . . . No? Well, it's a little early for me, too, but this morning I needed something. Christ, I can't get that other thing out of my head."

49

He waved them to chairs and poured another small drink, added water. He put it on the desk and sat down behind it, a plump, pink-faced man with thinning brown hair and a small, neatly kept mustache. The knot of his tie had been loosened and his shirt was open at the top, the sleeves turned back to reveal a wrist watch with a gold strap. As he slumped in the chair he put one heel on the corner of his desk and eyed it glumly for a silent moment.

"I guess you'll want to know about the business," he said. "Her lawyer called me this morning and said he'd like his accountant to go over the books. He said you'd inherit it under her will."

Such thoughts were farthest from Rick's mind at the moment, but before he could interrupt Eastman continued in the same brooding manner.

"Yesterday I would have told you you could have the business with my compliments because I doubt like hell whether there'd be enough assets to cover the liabilities."

"You mean you're bankrupt?" Rick asked.

"Not yet, but, brother, have we been skating on thin ice. If you want to know the truth, I've been looking around for a job. And you know why? Because of Frieda's big ideas. You know how she was—nothing but the best, big deals, a quality product, and a name for herself."

He took some of his drink and touched his mustache with one knuckle.

"Oh, she was smart enough in most ways. When we started we each put in fifty grand—which really wasn't enough capital but it was every nickel I had in the world. A couple of times her old man had to extend us some credit, but we survived and we agreed that I'd handle the business end and she'd be the editorial boss. No sticking your nose into the other guy's department. We knew we'd never have the biggest publishing house in town but we'd have one of the best. Anything that went out under our imprint had to be good—of its class. And that's where she began to go a little crazy.

"It was all well enough to print popular fiction and juveniles, and a few mysteries and good fact pieces when we could get them, but that didn't give her the prestige she wanted. So she decided to look for new material abroad. That part was okay. Plenty of publishers go to Europe to sign up promising writers; if they don't go they send someone. And they get some good ones. Some I know have turned out to be Nobel Prize winners and a lot of them have made money for the house. Sure we need those writers when we can find them, but that wasn't the kind that Frieda seemed to sign. Maybe she wasn't looking hard enough or maybe she was just horsing around. Anyway, with one or two exceptions that made a few bucks for us you know what we got?

"I'll tell you. Little items that laid a bomb. If we were lucky, we maybe sold eighteen hundred copies. We lost money by the barrel on those babies because no paperback house would touch them on a reprint."

He took another swallow and said: "The first couple of years we had our feet on the ground and we broke even, which was damn good for a shoestring operation like ours. Maybe we were lucky but we got a few writers who could produce regularly and netted a little profit on each book. We'd get a book-club choice now and then. We stayed in the black until two years ago and then she got this foreign itch and when she traveled she traveled on company money and not cabin class either.

" 'It's a legitimate deduction,' she'd say. 'Take it off the income tax.' But Goddammit you have to have the money the tax comes out of first, don't you? If we'd kept the dough she spent making those trips we wouldn't have done too bad."

"Couldn't you do something about it?" Rick said. "I mean, get her to cut down a bit or prove that her idea wasn't profitable."

"Hah!" said Eastman. "You were married to her quite a while, what do you think? She was doing what she wanted to do because she had her own income."

Crombie cleared his throat. "Will her death make any difference to your business?"

Eastman looked at the detective, head cocking as he considered the question.

"Yes," he said frankly. "Because now I've got a choice. We had partnership insurance to this extent: we each took out a policy for the fifty thousand we'd put in and paid the premiums out of the firm."

He switched his attention to Rick. "You're entitled to half of the business and you can have it all, and I'll clean out my desk when you say so and look for a job. Or, with that fifty of new capital, I can stay on as boss, hire an editor, and probably make out all right in the end. Why don't you talk to your lawyer. No hurry but—"

"All right," Rick said. "But that's not why we came. What we hoped to get from you was a little help."

Eastman scowled at Rick and then at Crombie. "In what way?"

Crombie took his Panama from his knee and placed it on the floor beside his chair.

"We're going to dig into her private life, Mr. Eastman. We're going to try to find out who might have had reason to kill her. We want to know who might have been in love with her, who she might have had affairs with—if any—who might have been afraid of her. It may take some doing but I can get plenty of men to help dig. You happen to be the first stop, Mr. Eastman, because you've been associated with her for several years and we figured you'd know as much about her as anyone."

He paused, his gaze intent. "It would help—unless you're in some way involved in what happened last night —if you'd tell us about your own relations with her. Were they always strictly business?"

Eastman swung his foot down from the desk and passed one palm along the side of his head. He glanced out the window and then back at Crombie. Finally he made up his mind.

"No. I was never in bed with her but I've got to admit I tried. Not in the beginning. We were pretty busy the first couple of years but being around her all the time—I don't know. She was damned attractive and when she wanted to she could charm an Eskimo. You could tell she liked men and not just for sex. She wanted attention; maybe it flattered her. I don't know how it happened but I fell for her. I'm not saying she sucked me into it, but pretty soon I was taking her everywhere and neglecting my family and thinking about marrying her."

He grunted softly, a bitter sound. "She never said no but she'd stall with that business of how could we talk about marriage when we were both married to someone else. Well, I knew there was nothing between you," he said to Rick, "and I was willing to ask my wife for a divorce. It went on like that for quite a while. I knew she was seeing a lot of Tom Ashley when she was helping him with his book. But she'd still go out with me, and be affectionate when it suited her, and stall me with half promises."

He waved one hand disgustedly. "But what the hell. You don't care about details. I fell for her, and my wife, who is no dummy, knew what was happening. She packed up with the two kids and took off for Boston. She's been with her family for the last six months or so and now maybe I can get her back."

Rick considered the information as Eastman fell silent. Nothing that had been said came as any great surprise to him. He did not know if what he had heard shaped up as a sufficient motive for murder but he knew that disgruntled and jealous suitors had killed women in the past and he found himself wondering where Eastman was around nine o'clock the night before. Now, remembering Ashley and his recently announced engagement, he said:

"If she did have an affair with Tom Ashley, how long has it been over?"

"I don't know. All I know is that Ashley worked out this last book by himself. We didn't have a contract for it and a few days ago he told us he was giving it to another publisher. That burned Frieda plenty. She was raving around here about his ingratitude and making threats about this and that, none of which made much sense."

"I've heard she's been seen around quitie a lot with Austin Farrell lately."

"I've heard it, too," Eastman said. "They'd make a good pair because they both want to be known as big shots. Only Frieda had some of the equipment and Farrell didn't." He shook his head. "But I can't see him chucking his wife—even if she is an invalid—for Frieda. She's got too much dough."

"Frieda would have had a nice chunk when she was forty."

"Sure, but that's over six years from now."

"Who else was she seeing regularly?" Crombie asked.

"Nobody that I know of," Eastman said. "For a while there Stuart Gorton was following her around."

"Who's he?"

"Another of our writers."

"Do you have his address?"

Eastman picked up the telephone and asked a question. A moment later he read off a West Side address and Rick made a note of it; so did Crombie.

"What do you mean, following her around?" the detective asked.

"I mean he was sending her flowers and presents and hanging around the office so he could take her to lunch or out for a drink." He grunted again. "But I don't think he got any farther than I did. He was with another publisher when she met him and I think she strung him along until he signed with us for two books."

"Can you think of anyone else?" Crombie asked.

"Not right now." He stood up and put the whisky bottle back inside the cellarette. "And remember, Rick," he said, "I'm not trying to prove anything about Frieda. She wasn't any bitchier than a lot of other dames; she was just too ambitious and selfish and self-centered for her own good. You asked the questions and you've got my answers. If you think of any others, come back again. . . . Glad to have met you, Mr. Crombie. Good luck, Rick," he added dryly. "I still think the cops are nuts and if you need a character witness, call on me."

Going along the hall seconds later, Crombie spoke to Rick. "That's a bitter guy," he said. "Either that or he had too much of that whisky before we came in."

Rick had no trouble with the apartment house superintendent, who had read the morning paper and expressed appropriate sentiments as he rode up in the elevator with them. Having unlocked the door for them he withdrew and Rick led Crombie through the foyer into a long living room that overlooked the East River and Long Island City. It was a handsomely furnished room, but it was the oil painting over the fireplace that held Rick's attention.

As he stopped in front of it he heard Crombie ask if it was all right to look around. He said yes and heard the detective move away and then he was studying this picture, which showed an old weather-beaten house that stood on the bank of a small, still river. The sight of it here in a place of honor touched him deeply because, though he had quite forgotten that he had ever done such a scene, the remembered circumstances returned at once. For of all his work this had been Frieda's favorite and when they separated she asked if she could have it.

Now, as his thoughts turned back, he experienced again in fancy the week they had spent at this small Connecticut inn soon after he had come back from Korea, the sketches he had made, the preliminary work he had done on this particular picture. He was still standing there when Crombie returned muttering under his breath.

"Two bedrooms and two baths, a maid's room and bath; kitchen, dining room, study, and this." He waved a thick arm to indicate the room. "Your wife didn't fool, did she?" He looked up at the painting. "One of yours? It's nice."

He coughed and said: "It would take too long to go over the whole place so let's just have a look at the study. Things you find in a man's desk are sometimes pretty revealing. Okay?"

Rick followed him into the study and over to the desk which stood between the windows, a walnut, kneehole desk with an inlaid leather top. Then, as if by mutual consent, he began to inspect one tier of drawers while Crombie set to work on the other.

Without looking for anything in particular Rick soon discovered that there were no handwritten personal letters or notes and he decided that it was Frieda's habit to destroy such things after she'd read, or answered, them. The top drawer held two checkbooks, an address book, which he put on top of the desk, some personal bills, charge-account statements, receipts. The middle drawer was filled with manila folders and he saw that the tab on each was marked.

One said: *Spain-Portugal*, and when he opened it he found carbon copies of letters she had written to the office while traveling. This particular period covered the month of April 1956 and he went on to the next which said: *France-Italy*. Here the trip had apparently lasted from mid-July to mid-August of the same year.

The first letter he scanned was addressed to Eastman and was strictly business as she wrote of arrangements with an agent and of a new French writer she had just signed. The second letter was written from Geneva and what struck him about this one was the date, which was exactly a year ago that day. In this she said she was resting for a few days and would go to Como for a few more. There were two writers in Milan that she wanted to see, and another in Genoa about whom she had heard wonderful things. The next letter was dated the 14th and had been sent from Genoa saying she had two manu-scripts about which she was enthusiastic, adding that she would be sailing the following day.

Except for the few words of enthusiasm the letters were strictly business and reminded Rick of the cards she sent him from time to time. Whenever she went on a trip he could count on one card containing some factual material and the style was more masculine than feminine. They began, *"Dear Rick,"* and usually ended, *"Best regards."*

Now, as he started to put the folder aside, Crombie touched his arm.

"This," he indicated the document he held in one hand, "is a lease for this apartment. This other one"—he offered it to Rick—"is another lease. Was your wife's maiden name Brainard? What's the rest of it?"

"Frieda Elizabeth."

"It's signed F. E. Brainard."

Rick skipped the printed wording and read the information that had been inserted in the blank spaces. From this he could see that Frieda had signed a lease for an apartment on Eighth Street, a two-year lease which had about six months to run.

"Do you know anything about it?" Crombie asked.

"No."

"She's had it a year and a half."

"I never knew she had it."

Crombie, who had been resting on one knee, pushed erect with a grunt. "Stick it in your pocket," he said. "Maybe we ought to go and talk to the landlord. It might save some time."

Rick put the folders back in the drawer and closed it. He picked up the address book, turned it over, put it into his pocket. He stood a moment, staring sightlessly out the window, his bony face somber and slack at the mouth. The fact that the existence of this Eighth Street apartment seemed to corroborate the things he had heard earlier served only to depress him. He did not want to go there, nor find out how Frieda had lived the past two years, or delve into the past. He wanted to drop the matter, to erase it from his thoughts, but the all-night session he had had with the police was still fresh in his mind and he knew he had no choice.

Now, with his mind made up, they left at once, and in doing so escaped what might have been an embarrassing session with the law. For as Rick started to enter a taxi a hundred feet beyond the apartment entrance, Crombie clamped a hand on his arm and said something under his breath.

Following the big man's gaze, he saw the two men swing purposefully beneath the marquee and into the doorway.

"Town cop," Crombie said.

"Those two?"

"The tall one."

"Oh."

He's probably working with some guy they sent down from the state police." Crombie grunted softly. "They could have cramped us a bit."

"But the superintendent will tell them we were there."

"So what? You had a right to look the place over." He moved into the cab behind Rick. "The thing is, we've got that lease for the Eighth Street place, and without it I doubt if they'll uncover it at all until you're ready to tell them. That means we're not going to be bothered for a while."

7

THE EIGHTH STREET address proved to be a narrow-front structure with a grimy-brick façade. Narrow stone steps flanked by wrought-iron railings led to a dim vestibule, the door of which stood open. Four metal mailboxes were recessed into the right wall with push buttons beneath them. A fifth button had the word: JANITOR under it, and some seconds after Rick pushed it a man came round from a basement apartment and up the steps.

A thin, balding fellow who looked to be about fifty, he was clad in faded khaki slacks, slippers, and a T-shirt that showed sweat stains down his breastbone. He came to a puffing stop, mopped his face with a bandanna, and eyed his visitors with a minimum of interest.

"Did you push the button?"

"Yes," Rick said. "Does F. E. Brainard have an apartment here?"

"Who wants to know?" the man said without hostility.

"We do," Crombie said, while Rick brought forth the lease and shoved it under the man's nose. "Come on," Crombie added and now his hoarse voice carried a brisk, no-nonsense inflection that Rick had not heard before. "We haven't got all day. Which floor?"

"The third."

"Let's have a key."

"Now wait a minute," the janitor said, beginning to bluster.

Crombie stepped forward. He did not move his hands but his paunch forced the smaller man to the wall, anchoring him there.

"F. E. Brainard was this gentleman's wife." Crombie said with a nod toward Rick. "Last night she got herself killed up in Connecticut—you can find it in the morning paper if you can read—so now he's taking over the apartment. Is the rent paid?"

"To the first, yeah."

58

"Then come on, open it up."

"Okay. Quit leaning on me."

Crombie backed off and the janitor led the way into a dim and musty hall and up two flights of stairs to the single door on the third floor. He pulled a bunch of keys off his hip pocket, selected one, fitted it into the lock. When the door swung open Crombie put out his hand.

"The key," he said. "Take it off the ring. We may want to keep it a while."

The man hesitated but finally snapped the key loose. "They don't give these away, you know."

Crombie produced a half dollar and handed it over. "Go buy yourself a new one. . . . Wait a minute," he said as the fellow started to turn away. "What's your name?"

"Tony Pelucci."

"Okay, Tony." Crombie pulled out his wallet and flipped it open to give Pelucci a glimpse of the identification but not enough time to read it. "We're going to want to talk to you after we go over the place and I don't think Mr. Sheridan—"

"Sheridan?"

"That's your tenant's married name."

"Aye." Pelucci clapped one hand to his head. "Sheridan. Sure. I read about that. Somebody strangled her."

"And what I was going to say is that I have an idea Mr. Sheridan will pay for your time if you want to cooperate. So stick around until we give you a buzz."

It may have been the suggestion of a fee that changed the other's attitude; it may have been the shock of realizing he might be remotely involved in a murder case. Whatever the reason, Pelucci was instantly co-operative.

"Sure," he said. "I'll be around. Any time you say."

When the door closed, Rick snapped on the light switch to get a better perspective of the room whose only natural illumination came from the two front windows overlooking the street. The rest of the layout was of the railroad type, with a narrow hall that led past a small kitchen and a bath to the bedroom at the end. Here an enormous bed stood in the center of the floor with a candlewick spread and a headboard wide enough to take two box springs and mattresses. The dresser, the chest, and the vanity were either antique pieces or excellent imitations, and as he glanced about Crombie said:

"Why don't you start in the front room while I take a look around here?"

Rick went back down the hall, considering the furniture, the scatter rugs, and the bookcase in one corner before he went to the desk, which was similar to the one in Frieda's apartment but less expensive. A hooded typewriter stood in the center of this. On one side was a leather-covered letter tray and on the other a manuscript box. When he leaned closer to read the label that had been pasted on the top he saw that it said: *Troubled Seas by Stuart Gorton.*

The center drawer apparently was used as a catchall and as he pawed idly over its contents he found pencils, ball point pens, paper clips, tissues, erasers, a lipstick, and a stick of gum. The right-hand drawer held some carbon paper and stationery bearing the imprint of Brainard & Eastman. The deep drawer was half-full of manuscript pages, apparently first draft material, since much editing had been done. Other than this the desk was empty.

Uncovering the manuscript box, Rick saw that the top sheet was a carbon copy of a note written to Stuart Gorton on business stationery, apparently a letter that had been written here by Frieda. It was dated the previous Saturday and read:

Dear Stuart:

This is to inform you that we are accepting Troubled Seas *as the option book under the terms of your contract. If all goes well we plan to publish it in January of next year.*

Sincerely

Out of curiosity to see what sort of thing Stuart Gorton wrote, Rick inspected the title page of the manuscript, but before he could read more than a sentence or two Crombie called to him from the hall. When he joined him in the bedroom the detective pointed to the open drawer of the chest.

A clean white broadcloth shirt with French cuffs lay neatly folded inside. Next to it was a leather toilet kit which was obviously a man's. Without a word Crombie led Rick back to the bathroom and the open medicine cabinet, pointing now to the razor, shaving cream, face lotion, and deodorant.

"It looks like Eastman had it figured right," he said, "and it looks like there was at least one more before this guy. Come here. I'll show you what I mean."

They went back to the bedroom and Crombie pointed

to a cardboard laundry box which was now open on the bed.

"I found it 'way back on the closet shelf. It was pretty dusty."

Rick looked at the two shirts which lay next to the box, one white and one blue and cut from Oxford material.

"The way it looks to me," Crombie continued, "these were at the laundry when the guy moved out of here for good. The laundry sent 'em back and your wife tossed them on the shelf and forgot about them. . . . Size sixteen," he said. "Thirty-three sleeves. A pretty husky guy."

"Yeah," said Rick and thought immediately of Tom Ashley.

"The other shirt is a fifteen-and-a-half with thirty-four sleeves. Who would it fit?"

Never having seen Stuart Gorton, Rick could only think of Austin Farrell. He said so, adding that Farrell was a couple inches taller than he was and probably twenty pounds heavier.

Crombie nodded. "Maybe it's time to talk to Tony. Have you got any money? If not I can slip him something and charge it to expenses."

Rick found he had a twenty, two tens and two fives. Crombie took the fives. "I'll get him" he said.

Rick was sitting in the front room when Crombie came back with the janitor. He closed the door and told the man to sit down. When he obeyed he swung a second chair near the desk and put the two bills on it.

"The first five is for your time, Tony," he said. "If your memory works okay you get the bonus. . . . Now, how often did Mrs. Sheridan use this place?"

"You never could tell. Maybe sometimes she uses it and I don't even know." He hesitated, but when Crombie's eyes stayed fixed he said: "Sometimes not for a week; sometimes two or three times."

"Sometimes she slept here."

"Oh, sure."

"Alone?"

Tony's glance slid to Rick and he pulled it back. When he hesitated Rick said:

"Okay, Tony. I know she was seeing other men. What we want from you is the truth."

Tony shrugged. "Sometimes she's not alone."

Rick's glance moved to the bookcase, and when a new thought came to him he walked over to it and inspected the titles. Two of these interested him and when he pulled them out, he saw the photographs on the back of the dust jackets. The first was a picture of Tom Ashley in an open-necked sport shirt, a pipe in one hand. The second photograph showed a thin-faced man with a brooding look and dark-rimmed glasses that had heavy sidebows. Rick had never seen him before but the book had been written by Stuart Gorton.

Tony nodded when he saw Ashley's photograph. "Sure," he said, "he used to come a lot but not for a long time now." His eyes moved to the five-dollar bills and he wet his lips. "He use this place more than she did. He work here plenty. I can hear the typewriter going, mostly when he is by himself but sometimes it goes when she is here, too."

"How long did this go on?" Crombie said.

"Three months maybe."

"And they stayed here some nights?"

"Look, mister," Tony said. "I got plenty work to do. How can I tell—"

"You've got your rooms in the basement, too," Crombie cut in. "And a couple of those windows overlook the front steps."

"All I know," said Tony, "is a couple times I see the two of them leave together in the morning." He gestured vaguely with one hand. "Maybe she come before this to have breakfast or something but I doubt it."

"What about this guy?" Rick asked and displayed the picture of Stuart Gorton.

"Sure," Tony said, "but not so often and I don't think he stay. Couple times I see them come in together but pretty soon he go away by himself."

"When did you see him last?" Crombie said.

"Not for months."

"All right," Rick said. "Has any other man been coming here recently?"

"One."

"Do you know his name?"

"No."

"Describe him."

"Taller than you and maybe a little older. Dark hair. Always good clothes. You know, dressed up. Not like him," he added, indicating Ashley's picture. "That one looked more like a bum."

Rick glanced at Crombie and the detective said: "How long's he been coming here?"

"Oh, maybe two—three months. Not very often at first; lately more often."

"What time of day did they usually come?" Rick asked.

"Mostly at night. Maybe once a week I happen to see them come in. Sometime together but other time he is alone and I haven't see her come in before so I don't know if she is here. Sometime I hear somebody leaving very late but I don't get up to see. So long as there is no noise or trouble, what do I care?"

"Didn't you ever hear them talking? Didn't she ever call him by name?"

Tony scratched the back of his neck and shook his head and then he stopped and glanced up obliquely. "Yeah, he said. "Once I am sweeping the steps and they go past me and in the hall they are talking about something and I heard her say: 'But Austin, darling.' Like that she said it."

The announcement confirmed what had until then been speculation in Rick's mind and he watched Crombie lean forward and push the two bills toward the janitor.

"Okay, Tony," he said. "You earned 'em. If we need any more help we'll let you know." He stood up as the janitor left and put on his Panama. "I'd better get something started," he said. "I'll get a man on Gorton and see what he turns up. Maybe we can find out where he was last night around nine o'clock. The same with this Austin Farrell. If he's a literary agent I can get his address from the telephone book."

He took out his wallet, extracted a card, and penciled a number on the back of it. "That's my home number in case you want to get me after hours. Are you going uptown?"

Until that instant Rick had given no thought as to what he would do next. Now he suddenly felt tired and depressed and in his mind there was only doubt and indecision and an over-all feeling of inertia.

"You go ahead," he said glumly. "I guess I'll just sit and brood for a while." He gave the detective a wry grin. "Maybe I'll think of something but right now I haven't got energy enough to move."

"Sure," Crombie said. "Take it easy. I'll see what I can get on Eastman, too. If Ashley is a neighbor of yours maybe you can do some checking on your own. I'll be in touch with you when I've got something."

8

FOR SEVERAL MINUTES after Sam Crombie had left, Rick sat where he was and tried to realign his thinking about his wife. The things he had heard in no way surprised him but they did force him to alter his opinion of how she had lived since their separation. Until the question of a divorce arose he had thought very little about her at all but now he had to think because it seemed likely that one of the four men most closely identified with her pattern of living had killed her.

When his eyes strayed to the open manuscript box he reached for it, wondering what sort of man this Stuart Gorton was and curious about what he wrote. As he scanned the top sheet a new impulse came to him and he put the box aside. For suddenly he felt very much in need of a drink and now he went into the kitchen to explore the cupboards.

He did not have to look far and he found that the assortment on the second shelf included Scotch, bourbon, brandy, and gin. A lower cupboard revealed a quantity of soda splits, and Schweppes, and when he had pried an ice tray from the refrigerator and loosened a few cubes he made himself a gin-and-tonic. Because he felt both warm and thirsty, he took a long pull as he stood in front of the sink and then, as an afterthought, spiked his glass with a bit more gin and topped it again with tonic.

Back in the living room, he pulled his chair closer to the window and put the drink on the floor beside him. When he had a cigarette going he began to read *Troubled Seas.*

The first page and a half, which set the scene, was smoothly done and put him on the water front of a fictitious island, apprently somewhere in the Caribbean. The focal point soon became a schooner tied up at the end of a jetty, and he gathered that the boat had been chartered by its owner to a vacationing group who had sailed it down from the Virgins. Holding the stage as the story got under way was the sunburned, steely-eyed young skipper and a busty girl in a bathing suit.

They were sitting on a hatch cover watching the rest of the party swimming near by and it soon developed that she would probably turn out to be the heroine because she was the niece of one of the older and wealthier women and had been brought along to serve as a sort of companion-social secretary with certain tasks to perform while the others had all the fun.

Until Rick got into the dialogue between the skipper and the girl he had gone along with the author. The illusion of the tropics had been skillfully done and carried conviction. The narration was interesting and he was ready to like the two characters around which the opening had been constructed. But the phrasing of the dialogue bothered him, though he did not know why.

He took some more of his drink. He read stubbornly on, his frown growing as doubt clouded his eyes. Finally he put the manuscript in his lap.

"For God's sake," he said, and now he read the next two or three lines aloud to see how they sounded.

Hearing the words seemed to make them worse and though he was not a great reader and certainly no connoisseur, he found the phrasing and words stilted, old-fashioned, and unconvincing.

"People get paid for writing this sort of thing?" he muttered.

He shook his head and put the manuscript aside, knowing this must be true since he had already seen Frieda's letter of acceptance.

He glanced out the window to find that dusk was thickening fast and obscuring the doorways across the way. When he looked at his watch he saw that it was after eight and he knew now why he felt so empty inside. He'd had no lunch, and though he was not particularly hungry, he knew it was time to get something to eat.

He looked at his empty glass and decided against a refill. He rinsed out the glass in the kitchen and put the manuscript back in the box, intending to come back after he had eaten and try another few pages just to see if his first impression would persist as the story progressed.

He still had the key, so he let the door lock behind him and felt rather than saw his way down the stairs to the street. This particular section of the city was not familiar to him, so he turned left and started to walk, coming finally to this restaurant on a corner and a block and a half away. It was a small, cheap-looking place with a counter on one side and a few booths at the rear about half of which were occupied. There were two men in working clothes at the counter and he slid up on a stool near the front end.

The specials listed on the board above the steam tables did not stimulate him greatly and he wished now he had taken the second drink. When the counterman slid a glass of water before him and dropped the knife, fork, and spoon, he asked for the chopped sirloin, medium, and a lettuce and tomato salad.

While he waited for his order he forgot about his surroundings and paid no attention to the conversational exchanges between the counterman and the two near-by customers who apparently were regular patrons. Instead he found himself thinking about *Troubled Seas,* and Stuart Gorton, and as he recalled the comments Clyde Eastman had made earlier he found it difficult to see the writer as a murder suspect.

According to Eastman, Frieda had used Gorton when she needed him, enticing him away from another publisher by devices best suited to the occasion. Gorton could have been a suitor at some period but apparently with little success. From things Rick had read he knew that jealousy was a factor in many murders and certainly an unpredictable element. But the fact remained that Gorton had still submitted his last book to Frieda under the terms of his contract. On the face of it, he seemed a less likely suspect than Eastman, who not only was frustrated in his pursuit of his partner but had been forced to sit and watch her push the firm onto the thin edge of bankruptcy.

But what had been the catalytic factor that had brought on murder at that particular time? What had Frieda done that made the guilty one—Eastman or Gorton or Farrell, or Ashley for that matter—kill last night instead of last week or the day after tomorrow? Or was this a matter of circumstance after all. An attack by someone whose hate or fears had reached the critical point at some earlier moment to be held in check until the opportunity presented itself?

The arrival of his chopped sirloin ended such speculation, and with the first juicy mouthful he realized he was hungry as well as empty. He cleaned his plate in an unhurried but workmanlike fashion, and while he sipped his coffee he inspected the pies that were displayed behind the glass case, finally settling for a piece of apple. A second cup of coffee and a cigarette completed the meal and when he went back along the darkened street his mood was greatly improved and a new idea was growing in his mind.

Instead of struggling any longer with Stuart Gorton's latest fictional effort, why not turn the manuscript over to Nancy? Reading was part of her job. To write copy she had to know the books that were to be advertised; she might even have read some of Gorton's earlier work. In any case she could give a sound reaction to *Troubled Seas*.

The thought became more intriguing when he understood that this would give him a chance to see her again for a few minutes, and such speculation left him rather pleased with himself as he fumbled with the key in the lock. Then he was moving into the darkened apartment and starting to swing the door behind him as his other hand groped for the electric switch.

In the brief instant that followed, instinct was no help to him because instinct was not working. So occupied was he with his own thoughts that even intuition had no chance to warn him. By the time he felt its first chilling thrust and sensed that he was not alone it was too late.

One hand was still outstretched when he heard the whisper of sound in the blackness beside him. There was a stirring of air, some unseen movement, a faint sound of an expelled breath that was not his own.

He stiffened in his astonishment but there was no time yet for fear and he said: "Hey!" softly, and tried to turn in the direction of this unexpected threat. He reached out, his finger tips brushing fabric, and with that his head was rocked as a fist exploded against the side of his jaw.

Off balance as he was he had no chance to set himself, and the force of the blow knocked him staggering backward. Before he could get his feet under him, one heel caught the leg of a chair and he fell heavily, twisting as he went down and striking on one shoulder.

More stunned than hurt he rolled over, and even if there had been adequate lighting in the hallway outside he could not have seen who had hit him. For the door slammed before he could turn, and as the darkness swirled about him and he struggled to his feet, he lost his bearings in this unfamiliar room.

Groping blindly as he moved in the general direction of the door, he knocked against the same chair. He spun it out of his way and ran into the wall, both hands spreading along its surface until he felt the edge of the casing. Then, aware somehow that he was already too late to take up the chase, he remembered that the two windows overlooked the street.

He could see the oblong outlines now against some outside light and he moved swiftly forward, dodging the furniture that was silhouetted in between. He put his head against the cool pane and bent his gaze obliquely downward. He could not see the entrance, nor the sidewalk immediately in front of it, but already some shadow darker than the rest had moved at the edge of the pavement.

A second later he was sure of it. The shadow became the figure of a man moving swiftly across the street, but it was a vague and indistinct figure, so foreshortened by the angle as to remain unrecognizable. Then, even as Rick strained his eyes for a better glimpse, a taxi rolled down the street, its roof light glowing.

It swerved and slowed as Rick watched it. The man stepped toward it. He turned to face it, and there was a moment when the dimmed headlights outlined his figure and glanced from a rugged face topped by thick curly hair.

That was all. The one glimpse.

Not enough for any positive identification of a stranger, but this was no stranger. This was Tom Ashley and there was some object under one arm that he thrust before him as he ducked inside the cab. Then the roof light went out and the taxi picked up speed.

Rick exhaled noisily and stepped away from the window, his fingers absently exploring a tender area along the angle of his jaw. He flexed it experimentally and knew that no great harm had been done. He felt along the top of the desk until he found the small goosenecked lamp and twisted the switch. While the room took on size and shape he walked across it and down the hall to the bedroom. When he turned on the light his glance went immediately to the bed. The laundry box that Sam Crombie had left there was missing; so were the two shirts which had been placed beside it.

So Tom remembered them, he thought. *And he's scared.* He went back to the outer door and examined the lock and molding. When he could find no signs of a forced entry he completed the thought: *And maybe he still had a key he forgot to return.*

Back in the bedroom, Rick took a final look around and turned off the light. He came slowly into the front room, head slightly bent and his brows warped above the shadowed, brooding eyes. At the desk he sat down and stared a while at the manuscript with very little in his mind but confusion. Finally, rousing himself, he put the pages back in the box and, as an afterthought, placed the letter of acceptance on the title page. He had replaced the cover and was reaching for a cigarette when he heard the new sound at the door.

He had no way of telling how long he had been sitting there or how long it had been since he had seen the taxi drive off with Tom Ashley. He did realize that whoever was at the door was having trouble with the lock and now, as he jumped to his feet, he snapped off the lamp and moved quietly through the darkness to the door.

He heard the knob rattle and then stop. A second of silence followed and then the sound of a key came again. Three times this sequence of sounds was repeated without success and when the fourth attempt clicked the bolt he drew back along the wall and flattened there, breath held and muscles tensing.

He saw the door swing slowly, the pale glow spread across the rug from the low-watt bulb outside. A slow-moving shadow reached out to break the pattern of this light and a man followed it into the room, his face turned away from Rick toward the front of the room.

The door closed and the darkness came again. The soft scuff of feet on the rug was the only sign that the man was moving. No attempt was made to snap on the overhead light and this spoiled Rick's initial advantage. He had expected that light and wanted to be close, counting on surprise to give him the upper hand should he need it. Now he could only wait for the intruder's next move; luckily it came almost at once.

For even as he stood there with a new uncertainty mounting inside him, the bright beam of a flashlight broke the darkness to sweep the floor near the front of the room and focus on the desk. The reflection of that light silhouetted the man sharply, a thin, not too tall man, bare-headed, the corner of his spectacles showing at one side. When he stopped beside the desk, Rick moved on tiptoe past the door until his fingers found the light switch.

The resulting burst of brilliance revealed the intruder with one hand on the manuscript box. He dropped it as he spun about. As he stiffened there with the flashlight still in one hand Rick let his breath out and felt his muscles relax. For although he had never seen this man in person he had seen his picture on the back of a dust jacket.

"Hello, Gorton," he said, and moved toward the desk, hands at his sides and the weight on the balls of his feet. "Looking for something?"

In his first moment of astonishment Stuart Gorton's thin bespectacled face held a look that was akin to terror. By the time Rick had come up to him a certain gleam of defiance had replaced his wide-eyed stare and his jaw tightened. He snapped off the flashlight but held it ready in his hand in an attitude that somehow made Rick think of a terrier at bay.

"Who the hell are you?" he demanded in blustering tones.

"Rick Sheridan."

"Sheridan?"

The eyes blinked again and the air of defiance was no longer so pronounced. His mouth moved but no words came out, so he swallowed and tried again.

"I—I didn't know," he said. "I wanted to get this manuscript of mine and Clyde Eastman said it wasn't at the office so I thought—" The sentence dangled with the thought unspoken and when there was no attempt to finish it Rick said:

"Why?"

"Why what?"

"Why do you want the manuscript?"

"What difference does it make? It's my story."

"Not exactly." Rick stepped past and picked up the box. He indicated the letter of acceptance Frida had written. "According to this, the story belongs to Brainard & Eastman. At least they have the right to publish it."

"What's that to you?"

"I may have inherited part of the business. Maybe not legally yet, but I'm interested enough to want to hang onto this until—"

"Oh, for God's sake!" Gorton's voice was suddenly exasperated. "You're not making any sense. I've been thinking about this story since I submitted it. I want to do some rewriting. What's all the fuss about?"

It was a reasonable argument and Rick might have ended it there and handed over the box if he hadn't remembered that Gorton had gone to an unusual amount of trouble to get the manuscript back.

"I don't know what the fuss is about," he said. "You submitted the story. It was accepted. Now, with Frieda dead, you want it back. You want it bad enough to break into her apartment. . . . No," he said. "I'm hanging on to this until I can turn it over to Eastman. Go talk to him."

He tucked the box under his arm and walked over to open the door, still not knowing why he was being so stubborn about this but determined to stick with his decision.

"Out," he said. "Before I call the police and have you pinched for breaking and entering."

For a second or so while Gorton eyed the open door he looked as if he might burst into tears. His face wrinkled and his mouth worked silently and then settled into a thin, mean line as his jaw grew taut. He started forward and because Rick wasn't sure whether the writer was going to give battle or not he got ready to drop the box and swing if he had to.

He saw the clenched fists and the hate in the bespectacled eyes, but apparently Gorton did not like the odds. He marched past without another word, continuing into the hall with determined, hard-heeled strides.

Rick closed the door and sighed, his mouth twisting into a wry grin because, now that Gorton had gone, he felt a little foolish about his stubbornness. He still did not know why he had been so intent on keeping the manuscript. He had no desire to finish reading it; neither could he understand Gorton's almost desperate determination to retrieve the story. *Why?* he asked himself, and when there was no answer he went to the telephone and dialed a familiar number.

"Nancy?" he said a moment later.

"Rick," Nancy Heath said in a voice that sounded both anxious and relieved. "Where have you been? I've been trying to get you—"

"I'll tell you about it in ten minutes if I'm lucky getting a cab."

"Here?"

"Maybe it would be better not to," Rick said. "How about that bar on the corner near your place? You know the one I mean."

Nancy said she knew and Rick said if she got there first to get a table where they could talk.

9

THE STREET where Nancy Heath had her apartment was quiet at this hour and the warmth of the August night had settled into the man-made canyon to leave the air still and humid. Rick had waited at the curb on the corner to see that she reached this entrance in the middle of the block safely and now she shifted the manuscript box under her arm and waved to him before she turned into the doorway.

For the past hour she had been listening to his story about Sam Crombie and the apartment on Eighth Street and the things that had happened there. She had no explanation for Stuart Gorton's abortive attempt to get his story back but she intended to read it when she could and see if she could find a proper answer. She was still intent on her thoughts as she stepped from the automatic elevator at the fifth floor and went along the corridor to her door.

Here she took the key from her bag and turned the lock so that the door swung open. Replacing the key, she stepped into the little entryway, aware now that the light was on in the living room but too occupied with her own thought to wonder if she had left it that way. She closed the door with her heel and leaned against it until she heard the bolt click in place; then she moved through the doorway. As she did so a man appeared in the doorway opposite. A second man stepped away from the wall three feet from her shoulder.

In that first instant she was too startled to be afraid. She simply stiffened in her tracks, her breath caught in her throat while the man in the doorway waved a short-barreled revolver at her.

"Stay quiet, sister!" he said and moved slowly forward, a thin, pale-faced man in a brown hat and brown suit, his eyes obscured by dark glasses.

"Real quiet."

73

The other man moved into her view and she saw that he was shorter than his companion, and stocky. He, too, wore the dark glasses but his suit was gray, wrinkled, and spattered with small stains on the front.

"Yell and we'll have to stop you," he said. "Just take it easy and you'll be okay. . . . Over here," he said and motioned her to the couch.

Nancy found her legs were weak but the stocky man had her by the arm now and she let him guide her. She felt him slip the manuscript box from under her arm and when he reached for her bag she let him have it.

"Get something to tie her with," he said.

The thin man pocketed the gun. "I think she's going to behave," he said and then grinned at her. "Aren't you, sister?"

Nancy sank down gratefully and when she finally found her voice her tone was more annoyed and indignant than afraid.

"If it's money you want you won't get much."

"Not money, honey," the stocky man said. "Just relax."

He opened the manuscript box and after a quick glance, put it aside. As he started to examine her bag his companion came out of the bedroom with a pair of stockings. When he separated and held them up she noticed with some satisfaction that they were not her best.

"Feet flat on the floor," he said. "Ankles together."

She obeyed and watched him wrap the stocking around her ankles and tie it.

"Hands behind you."

She twisted her body and he leaned back of her to bind her wrists.

"Now, do you want a gag or are you going to play ball."

"I'm not going to scream, if that's what you mean," she said acidly.

She watched him back away, his fixed grin revealing small uneven teeth. He rubbed the end of his long straight nose with the back of his hand.

"That's what we like in a dame," he said. "Co-operation . . . You find anything?" he added to his partner.

The stocky man had searched her handbag and now he tossed it on the couch beside her. "Unh-unh."

"Then let's keep working."

He turned and went back into the bedroom and now the stocky man pushed his hat back, glanced slowly about the room, and began to open the drawers of the table-desk. He moved confidently, whistling under his breath while he worked, and when he had finished he stepped to the chest next to the door, pausing a moment to inspect his image in the mirror that hung above it.

He continued his whistling and presently Nancy ignored him. She had not the faintest idea why they had come here or what they wanted but obviously they were not interested in money. Or jewelry for that matter, since her wrist watch and the sapphire-and-diamond cocktail ring on her right hand must have been noticed. Satisfied also that she was in no physical danger, she let her thoughts slip back to her talk with Rick.

From what he had said there seemed now to be only four people who might have had some reason to kill Frieda. Of the four she knew Clyde Eastman best because of her work on the firm's advertising. She knew that Eastman had been having trouble with Frieda and recalled an argument she had overheard in their offices but a few days ago. This argument took on new significance now. It supported Eastman's statement to Rick that the firm was on the brink of bankruptcy; it also furnished Eastman with proof that Frieda had been working behind his back by signing personal contracts with some writers so that she could salvage something for herself if the crash came. Making a mental note to tell Rick about this, she considered the three other men.

Austin Farrell she knew slightly and mostly by reputation. She knew a little more about Stuart Gordon because she had read his books before. The same association applied to Tom Ashley except that she had talked to him two or three times when she had spent a Sunday in the country with Rick. That he might have had an affair with Frieda in the past surprised her not at all, since she had known they had worked together on Ashley's second novel.

Now, as she considered him again, she remembered the noise she had heard in Rick's house just after she had found Frieda dead on the floor. Until now there had been no time to reconsider those frightening moments when she had forced herself to walk back through the darkness of the hall to the kitchen and the back door. She had stood there still too shocked and terrified to think but as she relived that experience it became so vivid that she remembered one more detail she had heretofore forgotten.

The car. Or rather the sound of a car that broke the stillness of the night.

She had heard it start up as she waited. She had not investigated. Her will power had not been strong enough for that and she knew that the car could not have been too close. She had glanced out the window toward Ashley's cottage, thinking the sound might have come from there, but there was no light to be seen and she knew she must have been mistaken.

But was she? Could someone have left a car there? Not necessarily Ashley but someone else. Or could it have been Ashley she had heard leaving the kitchen? . . .

She jerked her thoughts back as the stocky man spoke. His companion had come out of the bedroom and now he spread his hands in a gesture of defeat.

"No dice," he said, and the stocky man swore and gave a tug at his hat brim.

Nancy looked from one to the other, still not knowing why they had come but understanding that their search had been futile. While she wondered what they would do now the thin man came up to her and reached behind her to give a tug at the stocking on her wrist.

"It ain't too tight, is it?" He grinned again as he stepped back. "I told you you'd be okay if you made like a mouse. Five minutes, if you work at it, and you'll be free."

"She could start screaming the minute we leave," the other said.

The thin man was still looking at her. "You want the gag?"

"I told you I wouldn't scream," Nancy said.

"Okay. I took your word for it before. Don't spoil it now. All we want is a couple of minutes to get to the street." He glanced at his companion and jerked his head toward the door. "Let's drift, Al."

Nancy watched them open the door. She watched the thin one grin again and tip his hat to reveal his thick black hair. Then they were gone and she was straining at the binding on her wrists.

She found that the nylon stretched a little and perspiration had made her wrists slippery. A minute or so later she had them free and began to work on the other stocking. When she loosened the knot she kicked off her pumps and slipped first one foot and then the other through the noose. Finally she stood up, finding no runs in the stockings as she straightened them out and refolded them.

For another speculative second or two she considered calling Rick; then decided against it. She was still too puzzled to make any sense out of the incident and to telephone him now would only worry him needlessly. Tomorrow would be time enough. Right now what she wanted most was a cold drink and she walked stocking-footed into the kitchen to see what she could find. Not until later when she was sipping the drink did she change her mind about telling Rick what had happened.

When Rick Sheridan reached his apartment he found four letters in his mailbox. One was a bill, two were circulars from investment services telling him how he could make a million by subscribing to their bulletins; the last was from his son, and when he saw the familiar scrawl on the cheap envelope his heart was suddenly heavy and his steps began to lag as he trudged up the ancient stairs of the remodeled brownstone to his third-floor apartment.

Once inside, he put the letter on the end table beside his favorite chair and placed his jacket across the arm of the davenport. When he had walked through his rooms to open some windows, he loosened his tie and unbuttoned his collar; then went into the kitchen to get a can of beer.

Ever since his son had been in camp the weekly letters had been a high spot in Rick's scheme of living. He had made it plain that he expected such a letter even if it had to be a short one. He, in turn, had been conscientious about his replies and he tried to write every Sunday no matter what else was on his schedule. It was, he explained, the best and cheapest way for them to keep in touch with each other and to know what was happening, and to him the tone of his son's notes had told him the boy was happy where he was and liked what he was doing.

Now, as he slit the envelope and took out the two ruled sheets that had come from a cheap pad, he tried to blot from his mind the tragedy which had involved them both, to ignore its ramifications, to avoid futile speculation about the immediate future. The penciled and uneven letters told him the note had been written on Sunday and mailed yesterday morning, and the wavering sentences proudly explained that his son had passed his advanced swimming test and was therefore entitled to take a canoe out by himself. It told of an overnight hike some of the boys had taken earlier in the week in company of a counselor, and dwelt briefly on a camp dinner which had been given Saturday night as a farewell party to the boys whose families could afford the luxury of a camp for only one month. It ended as it always did: *With love. Ricky.*

When he had read it again to be sure he had missed nothing, he placed the letter back into the envelope and blew his nose. He took a sip of beer and this feeling of futility was beginning to work on him again when the knock came on the door.

Having no idea who might be wanting him at this hour and not particularly caring, he rose and walked to the door as the knock sounded again. He palmed the knob and pulled and then he stood right where he was, aware that two men waited in the hall but his gaze fixing on the gun which was pointed right at his breastbone.

"Back up, Mac! And watch the hands."

Rick obeyed. He put one foot carefully in back of the other and shifted his weight. When he could he brought his eyes up to inspect the man with the gun.

About Rick's height and build, he wore a brown suit and hat, and had a long straight nose topped by dark glasses. When he saw Rick would give him no trouble he grinned to reveal small crooked teeth. Only then did Rick see that the second man was a stocky, thick-necked husky in a wrinkled gray suit, his broad, lumpy face obscured by the same kind of glasses.

Rick was still backing because the gun was advancing. When he felt the chair at his hip he stopped. "What is it?" he said harshly. "A stick-up?"

"Not tonight, Mac," the thin man said. "We just want a look around. Take it easy and nobody gets hurt. . . . Turn the other way and clasp your hands behind your neck."

Rick turned and stood still. Behind him the door clicked shut and hands tapped his pockets lightly. The man with the gun moved round him, giving him plenty of room. When he spotted the jacket on the davenport he picked it up and tossed it to his companion, who searched it without comment and put it back.

When he continued on to the old Governor Winthrop desk his companion told Rick to sit down on the davenport. Rick did so, watching the other perch on the arm of his easy chair and reach for the can of beer.

"Still cold, huh?" he said, and drank from one of the holes Rick had punched. He continued to hold the gun in readiness but seemed confident that he would not need it and no longer pointed it.

Rick continued to eye him morosely. When he had seen the stocky man return his wallet without removing anything he knew they had told the truth when they said this was no stick-up. So what did they want?

Gorton's manuscript? Could the writer have had time to find a pair such as this and try to recover the story? It was a possibility but so remote that Rick presently discarded it and glanced over at the other man.

The room was sparsely furnished now, with most of his good pieces in his new house. There was the desk and the sagging davenport and two upholstered chairs that were comfortable but threadbare, a table, some lamps, and two straight-backed chairs. One of the bedrooms which he had once used as a studio held nothing but odds and ends; the second had little more than the two beds and a chest. Without the faintest idea as to what this was all about he said:

"Who're you working for?"

The thin man grinned again to show he was kidding.

"The F.B.I.," he said. "We got the word you were subversive. We want to see if you've got anything around in code."

"Sure," Rick said. "I've got a lot of code. Help yourself."

He listened to the man's chuckle and his irritation mounted. He found himself wishing the fellow had no gun. He had an idea he could take him before his companion could get back from the bedroom into which he had disappeared. For a moment he even considered the distance between him and the gun and wondered if he could make it in time. Then his common sense told him such an attempt would not only be risky but pointless. Unless he could make them talk, which was doubtful, why take chances?

He leaned back and stretched his long legs. For perhaps five minutes he studied the man through half-open lids, cataloguing the features so he could identify him again if he had to. Then the stocky fellow came back and muttered something about the place being clean. As he did so the telephone rang.

The thin man wheeled to stare at the instrument; then looked back at Rick, the dark glasses obscuring his eyes but his mouth tightening. At the second ring, he said: "Answer it. We'll both listen."

Rick moved to the telephone, feeling the gun in his side now as the man leaned close, letting him twist the earpiece so that he could hear what was being said. Then Nancy's voice came over the wire, her accounts quick and breathless.

"I wasn't going to tell you, Rick," she said. "I didn't want to worry you, and then I thought it might be important and I should tell you about the two men who were waiting in my apartment after I left you."

"Two men?" Rick half turned as he felt a quick thrust of alarm. "What did they do? . . . Nancy! Are you all right? They didn't—"

"They didn't do anything but search the place. They didn't take anything. I don't even know what they wanted."

Rick got a corner-of-the-eye glimpse of the thin man as he said: "What did they look for?"

"Both had dark glasses. One was thin, with a brown suit and hat. The other was stocky, with a gray suit, sort of sloppy looking."

"Yeah," Rick said. "They're here now but they haven't told me why—"

He heard her gasp. "But Rick! One of them has a gun. I'll call the police and—"

Brown-suit wrenched the telephone from Rick and pushed him aside with the muzzle of the gun.

"Don't bother, baby," he said. "We're just leaving."

He hung up and stepped back, glancing at his companion. Then he grinned. "Come on, Sloppy," he said. "Let's drift."

"Hunh?"

The thin man did not explain but spoke to Rick. "Thanks for the co-operation, Mac. And thanks for the beer." He opened the door. "Just don't stick your nose into the hall too soon and spoil it."

Rick watched them go without comment; then picked up the telephone again and dialed Nancy. The three minutes of conversation that followed added nothing to the solution of the puzzle nor did it furnish any answers to their common problem, and when Rick was reassured that Nancy had not been molested and that the chain lock was now securely fastened on her door, he said good night and told her he would phone her in the morning.

For another moment after he had hung up he wondered if he should call Sam Crombie. A glance at his watch told him that to do so would probably get the detective out of bed and it seemed now that the things he had to say could just as well wait until morning. He was still of the same opinion as he turned off the lights, went into the bedroom, and started to undress.

10

THE LACK of sleep caught up with Rick Sheridan that night and he overslept without meaning to. It was nine thirty when the ringing of the telephone exploded in his ear and he was still a little groggy when he answered it.

"Mr. Sheridan? This is County Detective Manning."

"Who?" said Rick; then remembering the round, bespectacled Connecticut detective, he added quickly: "Oh, yes, sir."

"The coroner wants to question you this morning."

Rick groaned softly as the events of the past two days came flooding back into his mind with a clarity that was discouraging.

"Where?"

"In his office in Bridgeport," said Manning and mentioned an address.

"All right. When?"

"Eleven thirty. Can you make it? . . . If necessary," he added while Rick tried to make up his mind, "I can get help from the New York City police to make sure you make it."

"Oh, no," Rick said. "Sure, I'll be there. Eleven thirty. Yes, sir."

He cradled the telephone and swung his feet to the floor. He yawned loudly and scratched his tousled head and then, absently, the fine hairs on his chest. Still not thinking too clearly, he understood that he could get to Bridgeport in time but there were other things he wanted to do first and finally he padded over to his jacket and found the card Sam Crombie had given him. Luckily the detective was in his office when Rick's call came through and he spoke first of the message from Manning.

"You'd better call Neil Tyler, your lawyer," Crombie said.

"Now?"

"Before you leave. Tell him where you're going."

"Oh?"

"Yeah. Because there's a chance you won't be coming back right away and you might want somebody to check."

"You mean they'll arrest me?"

"If they've got enough they will but if they haven't there's another way. They've got a funny law in Connecticut, a thing they call a Coroner's Warrant. A coroner can use it in a case like this. If he wants to hold you, brother you're held."

"Without charges?"

"Sure."

"Indefinitely?"

"No, but long enough for him and the police to complete their investigation. That's why a lawyer might help. . . . But let me know as soon as you can. I've got a line on Stuart Gorton—"

"I saw him after you left the Eighth Street place," Rick said, and went on to tell what had happened. He said he had no idea why Gorton had made all the fuss about the manuscript but that Nancy Heath was reading it now. "If there's anything fishy about it she should find it. . . . Also, I had a couple of callers last night."

Crombie listened without interruption to Rick's account of the two men and their search of his apartment.

"That's damn funny," he said. "They didn't take anything?"

"Nope."

"You got any ideas?"

"None."

"Describe them."

Rick did the best he could and Crombie said he would think about it and see what he could turn up. "Call me when you can," he said, and hung up.

Rick called Neil Tyler next and told him about the coroner and Sam Crombie.

"Crombie's right about the Coroner's Warrant," Tyler said, "and I've already been in touch with a young lawyer in Bridgeport who can represent you there if you need him. He knows that courthouse crowd and he's a pretty smart young fellow. Name's Johnson. Bob Johnson," he said, and gave an address and telephone number. "I'll phone his office now and tell him you're coming up."

"What's this coroner's thing going to be like?"

"He'll ask you a lot of questions and a stenographer'll

take down your answers. He'll be questioning a lot of other witnesses, too, but if you didn't kill Frieda—"

"You know damn well I didn't," Rick exploded.

"So the coroner and the police want to find out who did. It may be kind of rough on you but what can you expect? Just do the best you can and don't blow your top. Okay?"

Rick called Nancy Heath's office next and the word he got was disconcerting.

"She called about a half hour ago, Mr. Sheridan," the operator said, "to say she wouldn't be in this morning and maybe not for the rest of the day."

"She didn't say why?"

"No, sir."

Rick tried Nancy's apartment next and listened to the telephone ring eight times before he gave up. He was worried then, and trying not to be, and when he glanced at his watch he knew he had to get started.

He put some water on the stove while he shaved and showered. When he went naked into the kitchen the water was hot and he spilled a spoonful of instant coffee into a cup and burned his mouth with the first swallow. He took the coffee into the bedroom while he dressed and that one cup was all he had for breakfast.

He did not remember much of the drive to Bridgeport because he was still concerned about Nancy. As it was he was five minutes late when he found a parking lot a block from the address Manning had given him. This proved to be one of the taller office buildings and the number he sought was on the sixth floor. The two names on the door were NESBIT & BEALE; the other words said they were lawyers.

The only occupant of the anteroom was a round-bodied man in a conservative, lightweight suit. He had been looking out the window and when he turned to reveal the metal-rimmed glasses Rick saw it was Detective Manning. He made no move other than to glance up at the clock above a window which shielded a girl at the switchboard.

"I was beginning to worry about you," he said.

"This is a tough town for traffic," Rick said.

"Yeah."

Rick took a near-by chair and waited to see if there would be anything more from Manning. After twenty seconds of silence he thought of something and said:

"Did you find my wife's car?"

"This morning," Manning said.

Again the silence and though pride made Rick want to wait out the detective, he wanted information more.

"Where?"

"Across from the South Norwalk station."

"Which side?"

"Westbound."

"That's where anyone would park if he wanted to take the train to New York."

"He wouldn't have to. He could park there and take the subway under the tracks to the eastbound side." Manning crossed his legs and fixed his eyes on Rick. After another few seconds he finally offered some information.

"A taxi driver saw someone park the car there about nine thirty last night, or a few minutes before. He saw a man get out and start in the direction of the station. He doesn't know what he looked like, or if he went into the station, because he wasn't interested."

"Why else would anyone park there?"

"It's as good a place as any. Who's gonna pay any attention to him?" He pushed a finger at Rick. "Suppose it was you. You want to get rid of the car so it'll look like the job was done by some guy who didn't live in the neighborhood. You drive it down here because you *want* us to think the killer took a train."

He grunted softly and said: "You don't get a cab there at the station because the driver might remember something. But you walk two blocks and you can get all the cabs you want. You take a ride, not to your house, or even on your road. But you know that territory and how to get across lots. You give somebody else's address and you have the driver stop out front and you pay him off. He figures that's where you want to go but the minute he rolls, you take off for your place. . . . We're checking on those hacks in South Norwalk now. All of 'em."

He uncrossed his legs but before Rick could think of anything to say a door to the inner offices opened and Nancy came out.

"Rick!" she cried, her brows lifting and a sudden warm glow in her green eyes.

She had stopped so short that the gray-haired man who was escorting her nearly bumped into her. As Rick felt the sudden surge of relief and happiness at the sight of her he came out of his chair and Manning moved with him.

"I called your office," Rick said. "They didn't know where you were."

"Mr. Manning"—she glanced at the detective—"asked me if I could come out by train."

"And I can take you to the station now, Miss Heath," Manning said. "This's our coroner, Mr. Sheridan," he added. "Mr. Nesbit."

Nesbit nodded as he gave Rick a quick appraisal and Nancy said: "Do I have to take the train?"

"Will you wait for me?" Rick asked.

"I want to."

Rick said that would be wonderful and told her where his car was parked and now Manning touched her arm, as though he was afraid to have them exchanging any information at this point.

"Will you come in, please, Mr. Sheridan?" Nesbit said.

By that time Nancy was moving with Manning but she glanced over her shoulder and smiled before she reached the door.

The coroner's air-conditioned office overlooked the harbor, and a middle-aged woman with a stenographer's notebook on her lap was examining the view when Rick came in and was asked to take a chair by Nesbit. When he had settled himself behind his desk the man leaned back to make his preliminary comments about the purpose of the investigation and explained Rick's rights. His manner was businesslike but not unpleasant and when he was ready he began to question Rick about his movements the night of the murder.

For a while then most of the replies were automatic since Rick had told his story four or five times and, as before, he omitted only the fact that he had slapped Frieda and knocked her off balance. This was a conscious effort on his part because he did not want to make any slips. Even so he was badly jarred by an unexpected remark the coroner made while referring to the medical examiner's report. Rick heard this question just as clearly as the others but because he was afraid to answer until he had had a moment to think, he pretended he had not followed it.

"I'm sorry, sir," he said. "I didn't get that."

Nesbit eyed him directly before glancing back at the report.

"It says here that traces of blood were found in your

wife's mouth. I asked if you knew how they might have got there."

"You mean, there was a cut inside her mouth?"

"I didn't say that."

Rick was further disconcerted by the unremitting steadiness of Nesbit's gaze. He was reminded that this was not just a routine investigation. This man was playing for keeps and Rick hoped the faint shrug he gave made him seem unconcerned.

"I know you didn't. But I thought if there was a cut or—"

"There is no menton of a cut," Nesbit said crisply. "When I said traces of blood were found in her mouth I was quoting. Now I ask again if you have any idea how this could happen?"

Rick could visualize that slap without difficulty because he was still ashamed of it. He could almost see his wife's face as his palm caught her high on the jaw, almost feel the sting in his fingers. It was possible the inside of her mouth might have been cut, but he doubted it.

"No, sir."

Nesbit considered the reply for three seconds and put the report aside. "You were aware, of course, of your wife's inheritance?"

"Yes, sir."

"And the terms of the trust?"

"Yes."

"That additional income until your son is twenty-one will be helpful."

"Certainly." Rick could feel himself flush but he continued evenly. "But I've been getting along fairly well without it."

"How much will your income be—from your own work—this year?"

"Not as much as it should be."

"I beg your pardon."

"I built a house this spring. I spent too much time helping the workmen. I didn't get as much of my own work done as I should have." He paused. "Maybe twelve to fourteen thousand. Next year it should be twenty."

Nesbit glanced at his stenographer to see how she was doing. While he shuffled some papers on his desk Rick glanced out the window, his eyes moving from the tall stacks of a public utility plant where a collier was unloading at the harbor's edge to the point farther out with its tall radio towers and the skeleton of a roller coaster silhouetted against the Sound and distant shore. For a few seconds there was no sound but the busy hum of the air conditioner and he thought again about the slap he had given Frieda. When Nesbit continued, he went back to that same moment.

"Then on the night of the fifth," he said, "you had an argument with your wife, but there was no violence."

"That's right."

"The subject of contention was a divorce."

"Yes."

"Because you wanted to marry Miss Heath."

"Yes," Rick said and then, because the line of questioning goaded him into an elaboration, he added: "If I had wanted to kill my wife to get my freedom I probably wouldn't have waited until the other night. She told me a week or so ago she wouldn't give me one without a fight."

Nesbit's brows came up and he glanced down at his papers. "But according to Mr. Frederick Brainard, his daughter had decided to give you a divorce but insisted on custody of your son." He hesitated and when Rick made no reply, he said: "Is that correct?"

"That's correct."

"She asked for custody. You refused to give it. This precipitated the argument. Is that also correct?"

"It is."

Nesbit nodded, glanced at his stenographer and pushed his chair back. "One more question. Is it your intention to marry Miss Heath?"

"When I get clear of this thing and have the right to ask." Rick rose, started to leave, and then turned back. "I don't know whether this has any place in your investigation, but my wife had been running around with other men the last couple of years."

"Oh? Is this something you know or merely suspect?"

"I think in a couple of cases it shouldn't be too hard to prove."

"Are you willing to name names?" Nesbit glanced at his stenographer. "Please take this down, Miss Stevens, but not as part of the record." He looked back at Rick. "I'll see that Detective Manning and the state police are informed. Now then—"

For another instant Rick felt like a schoolboy tattling on his friends and then he remembered that this was murder and forgot his compunctions.

He spoke of Tom Ashley and Austin Farrell. He said that his wife had been having difficulty with Clyde Eastman, who might have had quite another motive for murder. He also spoke of Stuart Gorton but did not mention the incident of the previous night.

When he finished Nesbit stood up and bowed. He said he appreciated the information and thanked Rick for coming in. He said that when he had completed his investigation Rick would be so informed.

11

THERE WAS a heavy black sedan parked in front of Rick Sheridan's house as he drove up with Nancy beside him, and even from a distance he recognized it.

"Oh, Lord!" he groaned.

"What is it?"

"That car. It's Brainard's."

"Oh, dear," Nancy said weakly. "I wouldn't listen to you, would I? You wanted to stop for a bite on the way in, but no. We had to come here by ourselves so I could make an omelette—" She stopped abruptly. "Do you want me to drop you and drive around a while?"

"No. That would only make it worse. You're with me and you're my girl, and that's that."

"But—"

"I'll let you in and I can talk to him outside. Unless he wants to come in. Let him think what he wants to."

He pulled past the sedan and stopped in the driveway. He helped Nancy out and walked her to the front door, conscious of Brainard's inspection but aware that he had not moved from behind the wheel. When he had unlocked the door he told Nancy where she could find a can of Vichyssoise.

"The eggs are in the refrigerator but maybe we should wait and have a drink first." He turned back to the sedan and walked to the window opposite Brainard. "Would you like to come in a minute?"

Brainard looked him over with cold, contemptuous eyes. His jaw was hard but he no longer had his ruddy, outdoor look. The broad face was paler now and drawn at the mouth and he seemed to speak with an effort.

"No, thanks. I heard you were in Bridgeport to see the coroner and I thought you might stop here instead of going to town." He hesitated and his mouth twisted. "Even today you're still chasing after that girl, hunh?"

Rick felt the new warmth in his cheeks but he made no

90

reply. It would do no good to tell Brainard that he did not even know Nancy was to be in Bridgeport or that all he was doing was driving her back to the city. To Brainard this would be nothing but an excuse and a contrived one at that.

"What did you want to see me about, Mr. Brainard?" he said, and it came to him again that from the time he had first met his father-in-law he had always used the term Mister.

"I talked to the coroner," Brainard said. "I've also been talking to the state's attorney. I wanted to tell you that I'm putting on all the pressure I can to get you indicted for murder."

Somehow the statement and the obvious bitterness which caused it did not surprise Rick. Frederick J. Brainard was used to moving in a straight line once his mind was made up, just as he was accustomed to using his influence whenever he could. His daughter had been murdered. As yet no one had been arrested. Rick remained the logical suspect. It was as simple as that, and now Rick had no wish to argue the point. When he spoke his voice was low and controlled.

"If the police thought I killed her I'd already be arrested."

"If you're indicted, they'll have to arrest you. And there'll be no bail, no running around like an innocent man."

"I happen to *be* innocent," Rick said and then, to change the subject: "Do you know about the funeral yet?"

"The medical examiner hasn't released the"—he hesitated at the word, his voice breaking—"body."

For another moment his lip continued to tremble and then he stilled it.

"But I can tell you this. The funeral will be private and the burial in the family plot. You will not be welcome and there will be company police to see that you are not admitted to the grave."

"I have a right to be there, Mr. Brainard," Rick said in the same even tones. "I want to be there. But not if there's going to be a battle with your company men."

"Ricky can come. I want him to come."

"That'll be up to him," Rick said. "I've talked to him on the telephone. I told him I'd let him know when the arrangements were made."

"But you—"

"Ricky'll make up his own mind, Mr. Brainard."

Brainard's bronzed hands were hard-knuckled and ridged as he gripped the steering wheel. He was staring straight ahead, and beneath the bushy brows the dark eyes were wet and the lids were blinking fast.

But not because of what had just been said. Rick sensed that with those tears Brainard was mourning his daughter. It did not matter that there had been so little understanding between them. Since Frieda was eighteen and Rick first knew her he had never witnessed a scene between father and daughter that seemed ever to express any real love or tenderness.

She had visited him frequently, had come back to live with him briefly from time to time, but never with subservience. For she was, in her way, as opinionated and prejudiced as her father; she respected him but offered very little warmth or affection. To Rick it had seemed a cruelly matter-of-fact relationship, but for all of this Brainard's grief was nonetheless real. His sense of loss and subsequent emotional break-up could hardly have been more complete if she had been an adoring daughter and he a doting and affectionate father.

Understanding this now, Rick tried to find some words of comfort as he backed away. Before he could phrase them Brainard was back in character and the glint in his eyes gave them an almost fanatical look.

"All right," he said. "But I meant what I said about the indictment. If that fails, if I get the idea beyond a reasonable doubt that you killed Frieda, I'll take the law in my own hands."

Rick stared back at him, shocked not so much by the words as by the compulsion behind them.

"Yes," he said. "I believe you would. Even if you burned for it."

"I won't burn. I'm not above hiring someone to do the job." He stepped on the starter and let the motor roar. "With me it's an eye for an eye, and someone is going to pay."

He backed the car rapidly but Rick did not watch it. He walked slowly to the door. He felt no sense of personal alarm at the threat but he understood that it was real because in his present mood Brainard had built within himself a fixation that was not open to reason. Now, feeling as if he were a hundred and ten years old, he opened the door and saw Nancy standing there, her eyes anxious and concerned and her smile tentative.

She did not question him and for that he was grateful. Instead she held out one of the two glasses she had in her hands. "Gin-and-tonic," she said. "I thought you might want one."

He thanked her and there were so many more things he wanted to say that he said nothing at all. He watched her sip her drink, but she was avoiding his eyes now and her tone continued light, her nervousness showing only in the haste with which she spoke.

"I opened the Vichyssoise and I found some tired lettuce and a bottle of prepared French dressing. I don't want to put the omelette on until you're ready."

Rick took her hand and led her to the divan. He wanted to kiss her but he didn't. He waited until she sat down and then took the chair that faced her. He put his legs out and slid down until he was supported by shoulder blades and buttocks. He uttered a quiet sigh that sounded strangely contented and pulled at his drink. Finally a faint smile showed under the warped brows and his morose and brooding look was gone.

Nancy could do this for him. Just being with her was enough to restore a reasonable good humor under almost any circumstances. Because he loved her so he forgot for the moment his own troubles and refused to contemplate the immediate future.

"In a minute or so I'm going to be hungry," he said.

"You'd better plan to give me more than a minute. . . ."

The shrill of the telephone in the little hall cut her off and was echoed by the extension in the studio. Rick pulled himself erect and took his drink with him.

"Rick?" the voice said. "This is Elinor Farrell."

Oh, God, Rick thought. *The portrait.*

"Yes, Elinor," he said.

"I've tried several times to get you. . . . Of course I know what happened. I haven't been able to get it out of my mind, really, and I can't tell you how sorry I am for you. I know you and your wife were no longer very close but—well, just what can one say that does any good at a time like this?"

"It's all right, Elinor. And thank you."

"I know I'm being frightfully selfish to bother you now but I've been wondering about the portrait. I'd so much like to have it by Friday and I thought that since you said it was practically finished perhaps I could have it now so I could have time to frame it. . . . Is there still so much to do on it?"

"No," Rick said and, considering his last impression of the portrait, knew this was true. "As a matter of fact it might be a good idea to let you have it. Austin will probably find some little changes he wants and you may, too, and that way I can do the fixing all at once. As for the frame, I have one that will fit."

"Oh, wonderful."

"It'll do temporarily, until you decide what you want."

"You don't know how relieved I am, Rick. You're sweet to bother with me."

"It's no bother. I can bring it over"—he glanced at his watch—"around two if that'll be all right."

"Perfect. Austin's reading manuscript at home today but I'll keep him up in his study."

Rick had been watching Nancy and now he said: "Is it all right if I bring a friend in for a minute?"

"Of course. . . . See you at two, then."

When he hung up Nancy made a face at him and he said: "Now—now. It's only about ten minutes from here and we can go by the house on our way."

"All right," Nancy said, and stood up to finish her drink. "I can wait in the car."

"No. I really think you'll like Elinor. She's had a rough deal since the accident but she's still quite a gal. . . . Now what about the omelette?"

"Yes, sir." Nancy made a small curtsy. "Right away, sir."

12

THE FARRELL HOME was a two-storied frame-and-stucco house which stood on a slope overlooking a considerable expanse of landscaped lawn and, in the distance, Long Island Sound. A two-car garage, both stalls of which were occupied, stood adjacent to the left side, its driveway sunken slightly to give it less slope than the lawn. The right wing had been remodeled to give Elinor a ground-floor suite, and one window overlooked the porch so she could see who was at the door.

Because she refused to live the life of a cripple, she ran the establishment with a minimum of help—a gardener-chauffeur and a cook-maid, both of whom worked by the day, the maid leaving after dinner. When the maid was out or otherwise occupied the front door could be unlocked from the suite by means of an electric release.

This release clicked now in response to Rick's ring and he pushed the door open to let Nancy precede him before following with the framed portrait. Once inside he led the way, cutting in front of the stairway that mounted straight ahead to enter the large living room on the right. Elinor Farrell was sitting in a wing chair by the front windows and she greeted them with her friendly smile until Rick placed the portrait with its face against the wall.

"Oh, but I want to see it," she said.

"You will," Rick said, "when I decide where to put it." He touched Nancy's arm and led her proudly up to the chair. "Elinor, this is Nancy Heath."

The woman's smile came back as she inspected the girl. She was wearing a loose-fitting print dress with a white background that looked cool and comfortable, and her graying, dark-brown hair was attractively waved. There was a square of scarf in her lap and on the end table a book she had been reading lay open and face down.

"Come here, my dear," she said and gave Nancy her left hand to turn her so she faced the light from the

95

windows. "Let me have a good look at you." She glanced up at Rick. "So this is the one."

"This is the one."

Nancy smiled back at him, blushing a little before she ducked her head and sat on the edge of the chair that Elinor had indicated when she asked her to sit down.

Because he was a little embarrassed at such frank and open approval, Rick turned to inspect the room to look for a suitable place to show the portrait. He asked if Elinor was ready for the unveiling and she said she was, and now he swung a straight-backed chair with the seat away from the windows. He wanted to put the picture close enough to catch the light but not too close to his viewers. When he was satisfied he got the portrait, propped it upright against the chair and, a little self-conscious now, stepped back to await the reaction.

It came first in murmurs from Elinor and then Nancy. He backed up to get a better perspective, his gaze intent now as he heard Elinor say:

"Oh, Rick. I like it."

"It is good, Rick," Nancy said.

"Do you really think so?" Elinor said. "Oh, I know it flatters me but I like that, too."

She laughed softly and said other things but at the moment Rick did not hear them. He was looking at his work with critical intent and he saw a stately, handsome woman with direct dark-blue eyes and a dignified and kindly look.

Much of what he saw was right—the brushwork on the simply styled pastel-green gown, the arms and shoulders, the shape of the head. The highlights on the graying hair were good. But the mouth bothered him a little; so did the eyes. He had never intendeed an exact likeness, for he had seen the pain and the suffering and the courage in that face and he had wanted to tone these things down a bit. Now, glancing back at his subject, he wondered if he had overdone it; if he had made the mouth too gentle and the face a shade too full.

Without knowing why, he felt a twinge of disappointment, some small sense of the failure of his work, but he was too practical-minded to say so. In portraiture you did the best you could, but in the end it was the client who had to be satisfied or the result remained a failure. Now, aware that Elinor was addressing him, he remembered to smile before he looked at her.

"And you, Rick," she was saying. "Do you like it, too?"

"Yes, I think it came out pretty well. . . . Maybe a touch more work at the corners of the mouth but—let's wait until Austin sees it. Only remember." He shook his finger at her. "We don't make any changes for him unless you agree. Don't let him talk you into anything."

"Oh, I won't." She tipped her head as her fingers absently wound the scarf around one hand. "I really do like it," she said, and then her head cocked still more. "Oh—oh! I think I hear Austin on the stairs. Quick, Rick. Take it in the bedroom, will you?"

Rick could hear someone on the stairs now and her consternation was so genuine he laughed aloud as he stepped up to lift the frame.

"I've kept him from seeing so far," she added, amused at her own concern, "and he'll just have to wait. Put it under the bed, will you?" she called after him.

Rick was through the doorway before Austin Farrell entered the room, and when he had put the portrait out of sight he came back to find Elinor making introductions and Farrell shaking Nancy's hand.

"Hi, Rick," he said. "I wasn't snooping, really. I didn't know you were bringing it today."

"You're supposed to be reading stories," Elinor said.

"I have been." Farrell leaned one thigh over the arm of his wife's chair and took her hand in his. "Not that I've found much worth reading. What's the verdict on the portrait?"

"We like it," Elinor said.

"Then I'm sure I will, too."

"When you're sure," Rick said, "you can have it framed the way you want it."

Farrell gave a hitch to his yellow-linen trousers and reached across his wife for a silver cigarette box. With his long wavy hair, perfect teeth, and persuasive resonant voice he could easily have taken for an actor which, in a sense, he was, since he had a part to play both at home and in the city and seemed to enjoy playing it. Now, taking a cigarette, he remembered his manners, released his wife's hand and offered the box to Rick and Nancy. Nancy refused, but Rick took one and accepted a light. When Farrell had inhaled he said:

"What's going to happen about Frieda, Rick? Or would you rather not talk about it?"

Rick said he did not mind talking but he did not really know. He said that both he and Nancy had been questioned by the coroner, who was still conducting his investigation.

"If the police have any ideas they're keeping them to themselves," he added.

"They were here, you know," Elinor said.

"Who?"

"The police."

Rick peered at her, brows puckering and not understanding how this could be.

"The police came here? Why, Elinor?"

"They said it was just a routine investigation but they wanted to talk to me because I'd been at your place that afternoon."

"How would they know that?"

Elinor had put her left hand on her husband's knee in an affectionate gesture and he had automatically covered it gently with his own brown hand. Now her dark-blue eyes seemed perplexed.

"I thought you had told them, Rick. You must have."

And then Rick remembered and was suddenly embarrassed by his persistence. Certainly he had told them. Lieutenant Legett had made him account for every moment of the fatal day. During the all-night questioning he had gone over his movements at least twice beginning from the time he'd climbed out of bed.

"I'm sorry, Elinor," he said. "I'd forgotten. Of course I told them. What did they say?"

"They asked if I had posed for a portrait and when I said yes they wanted to know what time I'd come and when I'd left and if anything had happened during that time." She withdrew her hand and picked at the scarf as she dropped her glance. "They wanted to know if you'd been having trouble with Frieda."

She looked up at him and when he stayed silent she said: "I told them I knew you were separated but that it happened quite a while ago."

"Did they ask about Nancy?"

"Yes. And I told them I didn't know anything about her. I said I'd never met her."

"Thanks," Rick said.

"Well, it was the truth. . . . Wasn't it, Nancy?"

Nancy smiled at the older woman and spoke softly. "Of course, Mrs. Farrell."

Rick stood up, watching Farrell's handsome face and well-set-up figure as he also rose. He was remembering the apartment on Eighth Street now and the things he had found there, the janitor's description of Frieda's latest boy friend, the other things he had heard. Later there would be time to tell Farrell that he had given his name to the coroner as a possible suspect but he did not want to say anything in front of Elinor, who, it seemed to him, had already suffered more than her share.

He heard her thank him for bringing the portrait and made the proper replies. He did not look at Farrell again but walked with Nancy to the door and let her say good-bye.

Inbound trains were infrequent at this hour, but because Rick intended to come back to the country that night he drove to Stamford and parked his car near the station. When they were seated and the train was under way, Nancy, who had said very little, mentioned the portrait.

"I really do think it's good," she said and squeezed his arm. "I suppose you always have to flatter a subject a little."

"Women you do. Did you think I overdid it?"

"Not really. She *is* a handsome woman but I thought her face seemed a little prettier—or maybe softer—than it really was. I don't wonder she was pleased. Or does that sound meowish?"

Rick chuckled at the expression but he knew Nancy was right. It bothered him, too, that he, who was supposed to be good at likenesses, should have missed this time, but all he said was that he hoped Elinor would keep right on staying pleased until he got his check. Then, remembering something more important, he turned in his seat and snapped his fingers.

"Hey, baby, you never did tell me what you thought of Stuart Gorton's novel."

"No," said Nancy, her young face sobering. "I thought it was bad. Too bad, I think."

"What do you mean?"

"I mean he just is not that bad a writer. There must have been some reason—"

"What do you know about him?"

"Personally, not very much. He's about your age and a bachelor and I understand he's been writing ever since he got out of school. He tried a lot of things—some pulp stories and fact pieces, and radio while it still paid well. He did two or three original paperbacks and a couple of plays he couldn't sell. Then he caught on with Chase & Company with a story the dollar book club took and since then he's been selling regularly."

She puckered her smooth brow as she concentrated and said: "I mean he doesn't have big sales but he sells pretty well, especially to the lending libraries, and he does two books a year. Mostly love stories," she added, "with melodramatic overtones and enough sex to be reasonably spicy.

"Actually *Troubled Seas* is not a bad story. It's a professional job. The plot and the narration and description are good. It's only the dialogue that's so ridiculous and I think he made it that way deliberately. If the whole job was a stinker that would be one thing, but I think he wrote it that way so that when Frieda turned it down all he would have to do to make an adequate story would be to re-dialogue it."

"You mean, he wanted it turned down?" Rick hunched around with his elbow on the back of the seat. "Why?"

"To break a contract. I think he was mad at Frieda and he owed the firm a book and he made up his mind not to give them a story they would publish."

"But—Frieda accepted it. You saw her letter."

"I know and I think she did it for spite. I think she saw through his scheme and decided to make him squirm."

"The way he was carrying on last night," Rick said, "she succeeded. The guy was practically frantic."

"Because he was so pleased with his cuteness he never expected an acceptance. Actually it was a pretty childish move."

"For whom?"

"For both Gorton and Frieda but especially for him. If he'd thought about it with any sense he would have realized he didn't have to be panicky. He had a right to make changes even if Frieda accepted the manuscript. She could make it expensive for him—"

She stopped. She turned so she was facing him, her green eyes amused. "All right, darling. I'll try to simplify it."

"Okay," Rick said. "Gorton wrote a lousy story so Frieda would turn it down. Instead she accepted it. Take it from there."

"He owed the firm a book. He could not publish elsewhere or sign with anyone else until he delivered that book—or unless it was turned down, which would terminate the contract. Frieda accepted it, though I'm not sure why she wanted to spite him."

Remembering that Gorton had been the one who used to come to the Eighth Street apartment, but never for long, Rick thought he could name at least one reason but he did not want to suggest that Gorton might have been a rejected and embittered suitor. He wanted the rest of Nancy's explanation and listened when it came.

"Anyway," she said, "Brainard & Eastman would normally have the book set up. They would have to furnish galley proofs. A writer is entitled to make all the changes he wants but once a story is in type it's a very expensive luxury and the writer has to pay for half of the changes above a small minimum sum. Some contracts make the writer pay it all and that's why a pro tries to get his manuscript right before he submits it."

Had Gorton realized this the night before when he broke into the Eighth Street place to steal his story back? This was what Rick asked himself. Why had Gorton been so frantic about it twenty-four hours after Frieda was dead? To remove a possible motive? Could he have been so angry the previous night that, given the opportunity, he had strangled Frieda? Rick did not ask Nancy to answer such questions but he wanted to see Gorton, and he wanted to know more about Clyde Eastman. When he spoke of this Nancy came up with some information that suggested an even more timely motive for the publisher.

"I don't know too much about Frieda's personal relations with Eastman," she said. "But I knew the firm was in trouble, and not just financial trouble either."

"What do you mean?"

"It was Monday morning," she said. "I'd come over to get an okay on some copy and I was sitting outside Frieda's office. Her secretary was out somewhere and I was all alone when Eastman came storming in, and I mean storming. His face was livid. I don't think he even saw me and when he went into Frieda's office he was so mad he forgot to shut the door. He started yelling and she yelled back and for a minute I didn't know what it was all about. Then I knew why he was so angry. Frieda was getting ready to get out."

"Get out?"

"She knew the firm was nearly bankrupt and she had

signed three of the best writers on their list to personal contracts."

"What does that mean?"

"These writers were producers—bread-and-butter writers who had been with the firm and apparently Frieda had talked them into signing contracts with her. From what I could get she'd lined up a temporary job as an associate editor with some other publisher and was going to take these writers with her as part of her new deal."

"And leave Eastman holding the sack."

"Exactly."

"He'd have a bankrupt firm minus the three best writers and she'd have a new job. How did it end?"

"I don't know," Nancy said, "because about then the secretary came back and heard the row and closed the door." She put her hand on his knee. "And there's one thing more I've been meaning to tell you. It's about Tom Ashley."

"Ashley?" Rick frowned at the quick digression. "What about him?" he said, and then he was listening with mounting concern while Nancy told him about the car starting up while she had waited in the darkened kitchen after she had found Frieda.

Because her description of her feelings and the sounds she had heard were so vivid, he could visualize the picture for himself even as he understood that the car she had heard start up need not have been Ashley's.

Tom Ashley had had an affair with Frieda at one time. He had remembered some shirts that he had left in the Eighth Street apartment, had been so worried that they might be traced to him that he had come for them the night before, apparently entering with a key he still had.

He recalled the story Ashley had told the police as to his whereabouts on the fatal night—the dinner, the solitary parking of his car along the shore front while he thought about a story, his insistence that he had not been home since he left to get dinner. His house had been dark when Rick and Nancy had come home; it was still dark when Rick had stormed from the house after his fight with Frieda, the garage empty—

"You're sure there was no light in Tom's house?"

"Positive."

"You didn't see any car lights?"

"I only heard the sound of it."

"Someone else could have parked a car behind his

house." He paused as he remembered the country road that cut vertically off the highway and made a boundary for Ashley's property. From that road an old lane led to the back of the house and apparently served as a means of access many years ago. "But whoever it was would have to be familiar with that old road. He'd have to be sure that Tom didn't come back at the wrong time. . . . Did you tell the police that first night?"

She shook her head. "I didn't remember. I was too busy trying to give them the facts they wanted; before that I was too scared. And I didn't actually see anything, Rick. I couldn't be positive that—"

"Okay, baby," he said. "I'm glad you told me. I want to talk to Tom tonight when I get back. I've got plenty of questions in mind. Maybe he can answer them and maybe not."

13

WHEN Rick had put Nancy in a cab at Grand Central he found a telephone booth and called Sam Crombie's office. When he had identified himself to the operator, the hoarse and now familiar voice answered almost at once.

"Glad you called," Crombie said. "How'd it go with the coroner?"

"All right. I guess I'm okay until he finishes his report. What about you?"

"We've been working. I've had a couple of men going over Stuart Gorton's neighborhood and we've got a couple of things on Monday night."

"Good."

"He don't own a car but he uses a Drive-Yourself a couple of times a week and we located the garage. He took a car out Monday evening at six fifteen and brought it back at eleven thirty. He put one hundred and twelve miles on it, which is enough to put him in your neighborhood. Also, he had a girl with him."

"Oh?"

"A busty redhead is the way the garage man described her. Young. He didn't know her name but he'd heard Gorton call her Fran. . . . So we start working the little bars in his area because if he drinks at all it figures he'll have a couple he uses pretty regularly. Well, we found one and they knew him and the girl. Name of Frances Keenan. But nobody's sure where she lives and she ain't in the phone book but we can probably find her if we need her."

"What about Eastman?"

"I'm waiting for a report now but we know he was out of town on Monday night."

"He lives near Westport; he was probably home."

"We'll find out when—if we can."

"Austin Farrell?"

"The man who's in the country checking Eastman will

104

follow up with Farrell." Crombie chuckled softly. "This is going to cost you, you know that?"

"I'll do another illustration," Rick said dryly.

"Yeah," said Crombie and chuckled again. "Do that. You going to see Gorton? You want me along?"

"I can't afford you on an overtime basis. I'll give it a whirl on my own."

Stuart Gorton lived in a three-room apartment off Amsterdam Avenue and when he opened the door and found Rick standing there his mouth sagged slightly before twisting into a petulant expression. His pale eyes were hostile behind the wide-framed glasses, but in that moment of hesitation Rick kept moving and Gorton had no choice but to fall back or assume a blocking position.

Once inside Rick glanced over the disordered room, his eyes focusing finally on the desk by the window, the typewriter and stand, the pages of typescript that were scattered on the desk and had overflowed into the wastebasket. By the time he was ready for Gorton he saw that the writer was still holding the open door and now he said, his voice peevish:

"Look, Sheridan, I don't know what you want but it will have to wait. I'm busy."

"It won't take long," Rick said and then, because he knew he had to attack if he was to get any co-operation at all, he said: "I just thought I'd give you a chance to rehearse your story."

"What story?"

"The one you're going to have to tell the police."

"What?"

Rick waited, and for a second or so Gorton looked like a man squinting into the sun. When he had control of his face he shut the door and made another attempt.

"Balls."

Rick just looked at him, nothing changing in his face. "I had a session with the coroner in Bridgeport," he said. "I gave him your name along with some others."

"My name? For what? Why?"

"As a possible suspect with a motive for murder."

Gorton took a breath and his initial defiance leaked quickly out of him.

"You must be kidding." He hesitated hopefully and when that brought no reaction he managed a weak grin. "I didn't mean to get tough," he said by way of apology.

"But I really have been working. . . . You *are* kidding, aren't you?"

"No," Rick said. "If you want me to I'll sit down and spell it out for you."

He eased down in the nearest chair and watched Gorton walk over to his desk. He took a cigarette from a pack and lit it absently. He flopped down on the divan, a very worried little man in wrinkled cord slacks and brightly figured sport shirt that was unbuttoned down to his navel. He jackknifed one leg and hooked an arm round his knee and by then he was ready to argue.

"Go ahead," he said. "Spell it."

"I found out why that manuscript was so important to you. You thought you could break your contract with it and when Frieda fooled you, you got a little hysterical, didn't you?"

"So?"

"You hated her," Rick said, knowing he would have to play the rest of it by ear. "She wanted to sign you up for Brainard & Eastman and she not only was a pretty attractive woman but she knew how to handle men. She flattered you. She gave you a lot of time. She let you take her out. She even let you see her now and then at that hideout of hers—but never all night. She kept you dangling and she got your name on the contract and then gave you a gentle brush."

He hesitated while he tried to evaluate the writer's resentful gaze and then continued stubbornly.

"Maybe that wasn't so bad. Guys get brushed off by women all the time. But then you must have found out she'd had an affair earlier with Tom Ashley. You also knew that Austin Farrell had been seeing a lot of her lately and maybe you could imagine the rest of it. Anyway you hated her enough to try that childish stunt with your new book and when she crossed you up for spite you flipped. You worked yourself up into a murderous rage and you went to the country Monday night—"

"You're out of your mind. I went to the country, sure. But I was with someone."

"Yeah?" Rick said, knowing this was true but not wanting to give up. "Are you sure that alibi will stand up in court?"

The unexpected hum of the door buzzer saved him and then, by one of those miracles of coincidence that are so much a part of life's pattern, he got a break that made his trip worth while. His chair was at one side of the door and when Gorton opened it the girl who came in did not see him at first.

She looked to be about twenty-two and her dark-red hair was cut in a short page-boy bob. The cotton dress she wore had been rather snugly fashioned and now, with the heat of her body working on the fabric, the garment had a form-fitting quality that was something to see. The legs were well shaped, the hips firm and substantial, and there could be no doubt about the full-breasted torso. By whatever standard the term busty would be proper.

"Hi, honey," she said. "They closed the office an hour early on account of the heat. Is there any beer in the—"

She stopped as she caught sight of Rick. "Oops," she said, as one hand flew to her mouth. Then she giggled. "I didn't know you had company."

By that time Rick was on his feet and grinning at the girl's exuberance. "Hello," he said, playing it cozy. "Are you Frances Keenan?"

"Why, yes." The girl gave him a moment of open-eyed and approving inspection. "How did you know?"

"I've heard a lot about you," Rick lied and kept the grin going. "You were out in the country with Stuart Monday night, weren't you?"

"Fran—"

The girl ignored what was meant to be a warning. "We had a wonderful ride, didn't we, Stuie?"

"Where'd you have dinner?"

"At the Blue Shutters. Do you know it?"

"Fran!"

Gorton was a little desperate in his effort to silence her, but by then she was too wound up and interested in Rick's obvious enchantment to stop. And Rick, knowing an opportunity when he saw one, said:

"The Blue Shutters? Sure I know it. . . . Why don't you get the lady her beer, Stuie?"

"Yes, for heaven's sake, Stuie. I'm parched."

Gorton gave Rick a final frustrated and outraged look as he continued to compliment the cuisine at the Blue Shutters and then, abandoning the job of silencing his girl as already lost, he uttered a small moan and started for the kitchen.

"What did you have to eat?" Rick asked.

"A steak that thick." She made a space between her thumb and forefinger. "It was yummy."

"Was Stuie with you all the time?"

"Certainly." She broke her smile for a thoughtful instant. "Except for a few minutes. He had to go see a fellow that lived out that way." She giggled again.

"Stuie wasn't very hungry and I was," she said. "And he was through before I was and he wanted to know if I was going to have dessert and I said of course I was, so he said for me to go ahead and he'd be back pretty soon, that he had to see this fellow."

"And was he? Back soon, I mean?"

"Oh—it wasn't too long. I had my dessert and a brandy and a second cup of coffee. Maybe thirty or forty minutes. I didn't mind. I like to watch people."

Rick pushed for one more question, hoping to get a reply before she began to wonder why he was so persistent.

"What time did he leave, Fran?"

"Around a quarter of nine; ten of, maybe. . . . Ahh," she said and her eyes lit up as Gorton approached with her beer. "Thanks, Stuie. You're sweet." She drank greedily and licked her lip. "What's so important about it, anything?"

"Sit down, will you, Fran?" Gorton said. "And for God's sake shut up a minute."

The girl recoiled as if she'd been slapped. She sucked in her breath and said: "Well!" with an indignant blast. But when Gorton just stood there eyeing her disgustedly she flounced over to a chair and sat down so hard she bounced.

"Who was the man you had to see, Stuie?" Rick said.

"Don't call me Stuie, you nosy bastard!" Gorton went back to the divan and scowled down at his slipper. "Eastman."

"Why?"

"You know everything; you should know that."

"You were still scared your novel might get published the way you wrote it, so you went to see if you could get him to call it off."

"He only lived about five miles from the Blue Shutters so I figured I might as well while Fran stuffed herself."

"What did he say?"

"He didn't say. He wasn't home. That was about nine o'clock and there was a light on and I thought maybe he'd just gone out for some cigarettes or something. I waited fifteen or twenty minutes and then said, the hell with it, and came back for Fran."

"Thanks." Rick moved over to the door knowing he had done about all he could here. Whether Gorton was telling the truth did not matter at the moment. What was important was that it was about the same distance from the Blue Shutters to his house as it was to Eastman's place. "Now when the police check you out you'll know what to tell them."

"Police?" the girl yelped. "Say, what's this all about? Who are you?"

Rick grinned down at her. "Right now I'm a good friend of yours, Fran. . . . Richard Sheridan," he said. "I'm in the phone book. If you have trouble with Stuie, give me a ring."

As he rode down in the elevator and went back over the information he had pried out of Gorton by persistence and good fortune in the form of Frances Keenan, Rick understood that there was one point about which some knowledge was needed. Did Gorton know, could he have known, that Frieda was coming to see him, Rick, on Monday night?

14

RICK SHERIDAN barely made it to the offices of Brainard & Eastman in time. It was just five o'clock when he walked into Eastman's inner sanctum to find the publisher on his feet, his jacket on, his Leghorn on the back of his head.

"What's on your mind, Rick? I've got a train I'd like to make."

"We can talk on the way to the station if you like."

"No, go ahead."

"I found out some things since I talked to you yesterday," Rick said, "but first I'm going to ask you a simple question: Where were you Monday night between—say nine and nine thirty?"

Eastman, who had been brushing ashes from his desk, stopped brushing and his eyes came up. His round, pinkish face was still expressionless but his voice was oddly quiet.

"Why should I tell you where I was?"

"Because Frieda was killed somewhere around that time and you had a motive, a couple of motives."

"Are you out of your mind?"

"I don't think so. You must have carried quite a torch for Frieda to break up your home on her account; in spite of this she wouldn't go to bed with you. But she did with Ashley and probably with Austin Farrell. It burned you, didn't it?"

"You're damn well right it did," Eastman said with surprising candor. "But that—"

"And you admitted she had about pushed the firm into bankruptcy," Rick cut in. "What you forgot to say yesterday is that she also stole three of your best writers. She was going to run out and take those writers to some other house and leave you holding the bag. I guess she'd be liable for her share of any debts, but where would you be?"

110

Eastman began to swear. He did not raise his voice above a low monotone but he knew a lot of words. He walked over to snap off the air conditioner, a well-dressed and prosperous-looking man in a gabardine suit that had an expensive sheen. When he shot his cuff to get a look at his wrist watch Rick wondered how far the man would go to preserve his standard of living.

"Yes, she stole those writers," he said. "I don't know how the hell you found out about it but it's true enough. And now that she's dead maybe I can get them back. Is that your other motive?"

Rick had not thought of it that way but he admitted the possibility. "Stuart Gorton says he came to see you Monday night between nine and nine thirty. He said he waited a while but you didn't show. Did you know about the trick he tried to pull with his latest book?"

"I didn't read it, but after he got Frieda's acceptance note I knew because he came in here and started screaming."

"When?"

"Monday afternoon. Frieda wasn't here and I told him I didn't know what he was talking about. When I got him calmed down—that was a stupid idea of his if I ever heard one—I told him I'd talk to Frieda about it."

"Did you?"

He took off his hat and ran his fingers through his thinning hair. "She didn't come in. If he came to my place that night he probably wanted to find out what she said."

"So where were you?"

"Can you give me one good reason why I should tell you?"

"No," Rick said. "But since you're going to have to tell the police some story, why hold out on me?"

He went on quickly, using the same threat he had used on Gorton and quoting his conversation with the coroner.

"They've got a smart county detective up there named Manning," he said. "I'll lay you even money he or a state cop will be waiting for you tonight when you get off the train."

Eastman considered this a silent moment, his pale-blue eyes busy. He stroked his little mustache, put on his hat again and gave the brim a tug. Then he sighed audibly.

"I drove over to see Tom Ashley. I knew by then that Frieda was going to pull out and I knew that unless a miracle happened the firm would crash and I'd be up the creek. But there was a chance Ashley might be that miracle. His last book made a lot of dough—for him and for us. I'd heard his new one should do even better and I knew he hadn't actually signed with anyone.

"With Frieda here we couldn't get that book because Ashley was sore at her. But with Frieda out, there was a chance I might sign him because he and I always got along. He knew I did a good job selling his second book and I was going to put it to him frankly. I figured if I could get him and keep above water until that book hit the stands I had a chance to put this shop on its feet. And if I did, this time it would be all mine."

"Tom's place was dark at five minutes of nine," Rick said quietly. "It was dark about ten minutes after. It was still dark about nine thirty."

"It was dark when I got there around nine twenty, too." Eastman paused, his round face grim around the mouth. "You're not kidding about what you told the police?"

"Why should I kid? I'm in a spot and I'm grabbing at straws."

"Then I might as well tell you something else. Tom's car was parked out back of the house."

"His house?"

"His house. And if you want to know how I know I'll tell you. Like I said, the place was dark but I went up and knocked anyway. No answer. I don't know why I didn't let it go at that, but I didn't. I'd driven all the way over there and maybe I thought he might not have heard me and was sitting out back cooling off. I don't know what I thought but I went round there anyway to knock at the back door and I saw the car.

"That stopped me for a minute because I didn't want to be caught snooping, so I called out. When there was no answer I walked up—it was dark then—and saw it was Tom's car. It was empty and that was all right because I figured somebody—maybe the girl friend—had stopped by and picked him up. . . . You think it's important?"

A lot of things had been happening in Rick's mind as he followed Eastman's words and visualized that scene. When he tried to fit it into the things Nancy had told him he got no immediate answer but he knew that some time soon he would have to talk with Tom Ashely.

"It could be," he said. "I guess I'd better ask Tom about that and a few other things." Then, because he had run out of questions, he added: "Are you still taking that train?"

Eastman gave his watch another glance. "I don't know. You sort of scared me with that police routine of yours." He managed a grin but his voice had the ring of truth. "I think I'll knock off a couple of drinks first and think things over. If there's a cop waiting, let him wait a little longer."

He walked over to the door and opened it for Rick. He followed him down the hall. When the receptionist called to say something about a message, Rick kept on going. When he stepped into the elevator Eastman was still at the reception desk.

The dusk was thickening fast when Rick Sheridan left the train at Stamford, and after he got his car he stopped at a diner on the way home for a bowl of soup and a sandwich. When, a half hour later, he made the final turn which opened the straightaway on which his house faced, his mind was still cluttered with odds and ends of fact and speculation that seemed to clarify nothing and bring only more confusion. Even so his eyes were watchful as he drove. That is how he happened to notice the flicker of light in the big studio window.

It was gone almost as he focused on it and if there had been no tension in his mind he might have ignored it completely and put it down to imagination or some trick of reflected light from Tom Ashley's house.

He was vaguely aware that the windows were aglow here and that Ashley's car was in the garage, but his gaze remained riveted on his own place as he took his foot from the accelerator and the car slowed. Once again he thought he saw that flicker of brightness but he still could not be sure. There was no car parked in his drive or in front of the house, none in the little opening he called Lover's Lane.

And suddenly he realized that if anyone were in his place the worst thing he could do would be to turn into the drive and announce his arrival. He kept going very slowly, thinking, wondering, trying to make up his mind. Then something took shape in his headlights and he saw the car parked about a hundred and fifty yards ahead.

It was pulled well over to one side of the road with its lights out. More young lovers? Probably, but this time he intended to make sure.

As he neared it, he saw it was a small sedan and at least four or five years old. Without actually stopping as he drew even with it, he still had time to be sure that the sedan was empty. Ahead of him there was no house for another quarter of a mile and as he accelerated slightly a plan began to take shape.

He drove on to the next driveway, turned quickly and started back. When his headlights again picked up the rear of the sedan he pulled over as far as he could and stopped. Turning out his lights, he stepped to the ground and began to walk.

Another car sped by a moment later giving him a good look at the sedan and he knew he had about a hundred yards to cover. Not hurrying but alert for any sign of movement up ahead, he came up behind the sedan and noted its New York license number. It had been parked with its right two wheels nearly in a shallow ditch, beyond which was a grassy bank. He moved over to it and sat down so his view of the road ahead and his house was unobstructed.

He was not sure how long he waited because time was of no importance. He wanted a cigarette but was afraid to light one. He kept watching his house but from this angle the windows remained dark. When he finally realized that someone was on the road it was his ears rather than his eyes that warned him.

At the first suggestion of sound he slid from the bank to crouch behind the rear bumper. An instant later he could hear the rhythmic beat of footsteps on the macadam that grew quickly more distinct. Up ahead a soft but tuneless whistling kept time to the steps, and still not seeing anything, Rick waited, breathing shallowly now, his nerves tightly tuned.

He was ready when the steps stopped but still he waited. He heard the door open, felt the car rock slightly with the added weight of the driver.

Still crouching he moved round the left fender, his muscles loose and ready now but wanting the proper moment before he made his move. He heard the door slam. Only a step from the handle now, he waited until the lights clicked on and then he lunged forward, grabbed the door handle and yanked with his left hand. In a continuation of the same movement he reached into the opening with his right.

The rest of it was comparatively easy, partly because he

had surprise in his favor and partly because the man's weight had been tipped against the door.

Rick caught a glimpse of a thin, long-nosed face beneath the turned-down hat brim. He had time to think that it somehow seemed familiar; then his finger fastened in a coat collar and he heaved.

The man tumbled head first off the seat and when Rick let go of the collar he hit the macadam on the back of his neck. A startled curse was jarred out of him as he struck. His hat flew off and when he rolled over on his stomach Rick dropped on him with both knees.

He hit the small of the man's back with all his weight and the man groaned as the breath was crushed out of him. He struggled feebly a moment and then lay still and now Rick came to one knee and began to search him. He found a flashlight in one pocket and when he slapped aside the coattails he felt the bulge on one hip. The bulge was a revolver and Rick tugged at it. When he had it in his hand he stood up and stepped back.

"Get up!"

The man was still groaning but he could move. He rolled slowly over and pushed himself to a sitting position with an obvious effort.

"For Christ's sake!" he said. "What's the idea? You damn near broke my neck you crazy—"

"Get up!" Rick said. "Get your hat and let's go."

"Where?"

"I'll show you."

The man thought it over from a sitting position. Finally he reached for his hat and put it on.

"Why the hell should I?" he demanded sourly. "You won't pull that trigger."

"Probably not," Rick said. "But I'd just as soon belt you across the mouth with it." He reached into the sedan and turned off the lights as he watched the man come to his feet. "This way," he said. "We'll use my car. You can drive."

"Where're we going?"

"Back where you just came from."

The man said: "Ahh—" but he kept moving, with Rick one pace behind.

He sat in the back seat while the other drove into his driveway and then, still holding the gun in readiness, he unlocked the front door, snapped on a light, and ordered the man inside. Now, with a good look at his captive, he was certain this was the man who had held the same gun on him the night before.

"Where are your dark glasses?"

"Nuts to you, Jack."

"Empty your pockets."

"You empty 'em."

Reaction was working on Rick now and with it came a rising anger. It showed in the tight thin line of his mouth, the bleak and narrowed eyes. He took his finger from the trigger and fitted the revolver flat against his palm as his temper frayed.

"Okay, tough boy," he said and took a step forward; with that something happened to the man's thin face and the fight went out of him.

Apparently no longer liking the odds or the look on Rick's face, he retreated a step to keep his distance and began to reach into his pocket.

There was a small table near by and, still muttering under his breath as his last show of defiance, he put his wallet down, added cigarettes, matches, keys, a small notebook and automatic pencil, a pile of change. Rick waved him over to the divan and told him to sit down. He shoved the gun into the waistband of his trousers and picked up the wallet.

The identification card said it belonged to Edward Lynch. A photostat of a private detective's license said he could work in the State of New York and that he had an office on West Forty-Eighth Street.

"So—" he said and put the wallet back. "Who hired you, Lynch? And what are you looking for?"

Lynch had apparently recovered from his physical shock; at least his original cockiness was beginning to show through.

"I told you last night. I'm working for the F.B.I. A special assignment to look for secret documents. Are you a subversive, Mac?"

In spite of himself Rick felt his anger drain away. Something about Lynch's attitude and his outward indifference to his present situation was basically humorous and Rick found himself responding to it.

"I'm surprised," he said, "that a smart aleck with a nose as long as yours never had it busted."

"It's been tried, Mac. But you know what? It don't break; it bends."

Rick began to toss Lynch's possessions back to him and

as he did so an idea came to him which he embraced immediately. Taking out his own wallet, he found Sam Crombie's card and memorized his home telephone number; then he moved sidewise to the hall telephone so he could still keep an eye on Lynch. There was no trouble with the connection and when he had explained what had happened he got a quick reaction from Crombie.

"Eddie Lynch?" he said. "Oh, sure, I know the bum. Has a partner named Deegan. Deegan and Lynch, a couple of crumbs."

He described Deegan and Rick said it fitted the other man who had searched his place the night before.

"I still don't know what they wanted," he added, "but maybe there's a chance we can find out who hired them. . . . What I mean is, would you have a man you could send down to Lynch's office? Would he have a skeleton key or something so he could get in?"

"You mean now?"

"Sure. The office should be empty. If he could look around, maybe at the files, maybe we could—"

"You'll get in trouble, Mac," Lynch called.

"Shut up!" Rick said. "No, not you, Sam. I was talking to Lynch. . . . You shouldn't have any trouble," he went on as his enthusiasm mounted. "And if you do and there's any beef I can make a countercomplaint against Lynch. So can Nancy."

"Sure you can," Crombie said. "Yeah. . . . You're thinking pretty good tonight. At least it's worth a try. I've got a good man for a job like that and it shouldn't take more than an hour. You want to sit tight, Mr. Sheridan? I'll call you back."

15

THE NEXT HOUR moved slowly for Rick Sheridan. He sat down opposite Lynch but for a long time nobody said anything. From time to time they would look at each other and then, like subway riders, they would shift their gazes to the walls, the pictures, the pieces of furniture. Finally, as he ground out his second cigarette, Lynch said:

"Hey, Mac! How's chances for a drink? You're not on the wagon, are you?"

Rick eyed him wearily, inspecting again the long thin nose, the prominent ears, the sallow skin.

"What have you got in mind?"

"Whatever you say. I'm only a guest here."

"Would you settle for a beer?"

"If that's the best you can do."

Rick stood up and pulled out the revolver. He was no longer annoyed by Lynch but neither did he trust him and he did not want to get jumped when he wasn't looking. He pointed the gun.

"In the kitchen," he said, and followed the man to the refrigerator. He stood aside while Lynch brought forth two cans, told him where the opener was.

Back in the living room they resumed their seats and the silence began to build again. From time to time a match would scratch, there would be a sound of drinking and the rap of a can being replaced. After a particularly long silence Lynch sighed.

"How come no television?" he said. "You know something, Mac? You're a pretty dull guy. How much longer do I have to park here?"

"I don't know. Maybe I've got plans for you."

"Like what?"

"Like calling the state police."

"Wait a minute." Lynch sat up, his face sagging. "You wouldn't do that. I said you were a dull guy, not a rat."

This time the bell saved him and when Rick picked up the telephone Sam Crombie's low hoarse voice gave forth with information.

"No trouble, Mr. Sheridan. A quick once-over of their files didn't turn up anything on any of the names we're interested in but we did find one thing that looks like a lead."

"Good."

"In the center drawer of a desk we found a receipt book. You know, the kind a man would use to have a record of his retainers or payments. The client gets the original, the carbon stays in the book. Well, the top carbon is a receipt for two hundred bucks. It's dated Tuesday, the 6th. It's marked: *Retainer from A. Farrell* and is signed by Lynch."

"Ahh—" said Rick.

"Yeah. We'd better step up the work on Farrell tomorrow. Did you talk to Ashley yet?"

"I'm going to later. What do I do with Lynch?"

Crombie chuckled. "That's up to you, Mr. Sheridan. He's your boy. Maybe, since we've got what we want and no harm was done—or unless you're sore at him—you could just tell him to beat it."

Rick thanked him and hung up. Lynch was still sitting erect and his eyes were anxious. "What did he say?"

"He said you were working for Austin Farrell."

"What did he say about me?"

"He said you were a bum and I could use my own judgment. Now what did Farrell want with you? What did he ask you to get?"

Lynch took a deep breath and held it. He leaned back on the cushion and folded his arms in an attitude of utter resignation.

"Go ahead," he said. "Call the cops if you want."

Rick hesitated, but not for long. Somehow he seemed to know he would get no answers from Lynch and that threats would be useless. Under the circumstances he did not think the police could do much better, so he said:

"Okay, tough boy. Take a walk."

He watched the sallow face break into a relieved grin. Then, as though afraid Rick would change his mind, Lynch jumped to his feet, let out a groan as he clutched the small of his back, and straightened with an effort.

"You know something," he said, still grimacing. "You damn near broke my back."

But he kept moving and he was halfway to the door when he turned, his eyes again crafty.

"How about the gun, Mac?"

Rick glanced down at it. "I guess you wouldn't be much good without it, would you?"

"It sometimes helps scare people."

Rick flipped out the cylinder and dumped the shells into his palm. He tossed the revolver and Lynch caught it expertly, saluted with it, and opened the door. When the telephone began to ring again, he went out fast.

This time the voice was a man's but Rick did not recognize it. "Yes," he said. "This is Mr. Sheridan."

"I'm Bob Johnson."

"Who?"

"Bob Johnson." There was a pause. "Neil Tyler called me this morning and said you might need a lawyer in—"

"Oh, yes," Rick said. "Sure. I'm sorry. I meant to get in touch with you but—"

"That's okay. I've been doing a little spadework and I came up with something I thought you'd like to know. Frederick Brainard's been exerting a lot of pressure here and there and I heard that Alan Oakes, he's the state's attorney, is going before Judge Sitwell tomorrow to ask that a grand jury be impaneled and try to get an indictment."

"Oh—oh," Rick said. "Does that mean the police have got some new evidence against me?"

"Not necessarily. The way I get it Oakes would rather wait. But with Brainard on his neck he probably figures he can make the move and leave it up to the grand jury. Then, whether they return a true bill or not, he'll be in the clear. Temporarily, at least."

Rick was not sure what all this meant but it sounded bad and as he hesitated all the old worries and pressures came back to assail him.

"What happens with a grand jury anyway?"

"Well, in this state a grand jury is only called—I'm not speaking of federal grand juries now—when the case involves a man's life or life imprisonment. That means first or second degree murder, plus a new bill dealing with certain narcotic cases. If the grand jury indicts you, you'll go to jail to await trial, probably without bail."

"What happens if they don't indict?"

"Nothing much. You can still be arrested when and if

the police think they have a better case. With new evidence, whenever it comes to light, another grand jury will be impaneled. They can indict if they think there is probable cause."

"But—don't I have to be notified? I mean, can they just go ahead and indict me without—"

"In this state the accused is usually present, but in an old case—the State against Wolcott—it was held that a grand jury need give no notice of proceedings to the accused, and that it could originate charges without notice to offender."

"That's great," Rick said dejectedly. "Then there's nothing I can do about it."

"Just hope the police turn up the actual killer."

"How long will it take to call a grand jury and get it working?"

"I'd say you shouldn't make any plans after the day after tomorrow. But there's no point in worrying about it now. You can get me any time either at the office or here at home. Meanwhile I'll keep in touch with things."

Rick thanked him and cradled the telephone. He pushed away from the wall and started for the door, knowing that he may already have waited too long before talking with Tom Ashley.

The night was still and starlit as Rick walked along the edge of the road, wondering what he was going to say to Ashley and how he was going to start. For he and Ashley had been pretty good friends since that night Rick had come here as a guest. Their backgrounds and interests were dissimilar but they had the war in common—Ashley had been a Marine corporal in the Pacific—and as neighbors they were on the best of terms.

The story-and-a-half house stood rather close to the road and in modernizing it Ashley had knocked out some partitions and added others. One front corner held the kitchen and a dining nook; across the narrow front hall and the stairs that led to the two bedrooms above was the study, leaving the entire rear of the house as one big living room. Now, seeing a light in the study, Rick knocked at the front door. It stood open and presently Ashley came to hold the screen door.

"Hi, Rick," he said. "I've been wondering about you. Tried to get you a couple of times—"

"I was in the city most of the day."

Rick followed Ashley into the study which was pine paneled, squarish, and had a small fireplace. Except for this and the two multiple-paned windows the rest of the walls were bookshelves, well filled now. There was a small antique desk, its chair, and two leather chairs. On the drop-leaf table was a bottle of bourbon, a thermos jug, and a pitcher of water. One oversized Old Fashioned glass, nearly empty now, stood at one side and Ashley drained it.

"I'll get another glass," he said.

When he came back and put some ice cubes in both glasses Rick decided he might as well make his position clear. He started by asking if the police had been around.

"Hah! They've been around. I was down there with 'em four hours this afternoon."

"Did they say why?"

"They said they'd got some new information."

"They got the idea from me," Rick said. "I told the coroner this morning and I guess he passed the word around."

Ashley had been pouring whisky. Now, still holding the bottle and glass up in front of him, he turned his head.

"So you're the one that blew the whistle on me?" He finished his pouring and if he was annoyed he gave no sign. "Why?"

"I was their number-one boy. But I didn't kill her. I told the coroner there were some other guys around with motives."

"Including me."

He handed Rick the drink and made a fresh one for himself. When he had tasted it he took a straight-stemmed pipe from a rack and began to fill it from a humidor. His curly hair looked dark and thick in the lamplight and the deep tan of his powerful neck contrasted sharply with the white T-shirt which was tight across the chest and shoulders. When he had his pipe drawing well he sat down and crossed his knees, his broad face impassive, his dark eyes intent.

"How do you figure it?" he asked finally.

"There are several things," Rick said. "What did you clip me with last night down in the Eighth Street place, a right or a left?"

Ashley took four tiny puffs in the center of his lips and shook his head. "You must be on another wave length, kid. I don't get your signal."

"That apartment has front windows," Rick said. "I saw you flag the cab. . . . With that laundry box under your arm."

"Okay." Ashley waved the pipe in the air. "I had to be sure. I didn't hurt you, did I?"

"I guess you figured someone would eventually get around to checking that apartment. If they did they'd find the shirts and trace the laundry mark to you."

"Something like that. Suppose you lay it on the line. All of it."

Rick took a swallow of his drink and reached for a cigarette. "Okay, Tom. Let's start with your affair with Frieda. You don't deny that, do you?"

"No. And if it's all right with you I'll tell you about it." He settled deeper in his chair and put his head back, his gaze on the ceiling and one hand cuddling the pipe. "I never had much of a family and none of 'em had a dime. At that I got through high school and the hitch in the Marines taught me the value of an education. I did a lot of reading when I could and a spell in a hospital gave me the time.

"I started to write a little. You know, experiences, things I heard, sketches of some of the guys I knew. When I got out I kicked around the Midwest working at this and that. I also went to night school and a teacher I had liked the way I wrote and gave me some help. Later when I came to New York I got a job as a counterman and took some more courses and kept writing. Finally I had a book, or what I thought was a book. Somebody sent me to Austin Farrell and he said he couldn't handle it as it was but he told me to go see Frieda."

He blew smoke at the ceiling and said: "The firm had only been going for a couple of years and they were looking for new writers and I guess Frieda thought I had something. She gave me a lot of criticism. She made me rewrite and rewrite and when I got discouraged she'd needle me. Anyway she finally decided to publish it but she made me promise I'd do another one. I didn't have to hurry. I had to get the right idea first, but I had to stick with it. I discussed a lot of ideas with her before we decided I had the right one and I started in all over again. . . . About that time she got that apartment on Eighth Street and I was only working about two blocks from there so she let me use it—"

He broke off and reached for his glass. "But you don't

care about details. Let's say we worked together so often that we sort of fell for each other, but I can tell you this: Frieda was not a promiscuous woman. She told me—and I believed her—that until we had this affair there had never been any other man but you."

He hesitated, glance averted and searching for some words. "I have an idea there hasn't been anyone since until Austin Farrell came into the picture. I know neither Gorton nor Eastman could get to first base that way and I doubt if anyone else did. She just wasn't that kind. . . . And this I can say: I owed her plenty. Not just for making a writer out of me five years earlier than I could ever have made it without her but by teaching me manners and smoothing off the rough edges and giving me a chance to be somebody. On the other hand she was the most selfish, opinionated, critical, and hard-to-get-along-with woman I've ever known. That was all to the good when she was making me write, but how can you love a dame who is always cracking a whip?

"The second book did well. When we were out together—she always had to have somebody drag her around—she sort of put me on display with her friends, but it was always do this, do that. If I forgot to light her cigarette or didn't respond to her mood the way she thought I should she'd sulk for three days. Then I'd get sore and not see her for a while and then she'd call me up again. All the time I was trying to work on the new book and I couldn't concentrate because I was always on edge about her. Well, we'd been having these little fights and finally we had the big one and I knew this was no good. I couldn't take it any longer so I holed up in a West Side hotel room and started to work. I didn't see her, or hardly anyone else, for three or four months—until I got a rough draft done. I showed it to my agent—"

"Farrell?" Rick asked.

"No, not Farrell. I never went back to him. He only plays at the job anyway. . . . Where was I? Oh, yeah. Well, while I'm rewriting, the word gets out I've got another good story and one day Frieda calls me and asks when she's going to get the manuscript. Now, in the first place I didn't have a contract with her for that book; in the scond, she's got that tone of voice that burns a guy because it sounds as if you'd better get it over there on the double or she won't take it at all. So I said I didn't have a contract, and she said what difference did that make, she discovered me, didn't she?"

He grunted shortly and glanced at his pipe. When he found it was out he put it aside.

"The hell of it is," he said honestly, "she was right. If she'd just been nice about it and maybe let me think I was doing her a favor I might have gone along with her. But a guy doesn't always want his nose rubbed in the truth, does he? Especially if maybe he's got a little guilty conscience. Well, this time she snapped at me in that demanding way of hers and I snapped back and the first thing I knew we were both yelling and I never could talk her down. I made up my mind she wasn't going to get that book and hung up on her.

"By that time I'd met Helen and was halfway in love. Later when I realized she was in love with me—well, it was just one of those wonderful things you never think can happen to you. Her folks liked me and her friends liked me and for the first time in my life I felt at ease with people I wanted to be with. Everything was perfect. We're going to get married next month. And then a week ago Frieda lays it on the line. She's like an elephant with a grudge. She wants to publish this new book. The firm needs it and either I deliver or she lowers the boom."

"About the fact that you'd had an affair with her?" Rick said.

"Not just that," he said bleakly. "That I could have handled because Helen knows I'm no saint. But there was another thing. I had a little trouble with the law once. . . . A long time ago I did thirty days with sixty suspended and a year's probation—which I violated. And one night Frieda and I are together. We'd been drinking a bit and we're there in the dark talking quiet about this and that and when I've a few too many my tongue loosens up."

He looked at his empty glass and moved over to make a fresh drink. "I talk too much, especially if I like a person. Maybe I'm talking too much now; I know I talked too much that night. So Frieda's going to make sure Helen knows the score about me and the law and I don't want that to happen. I'm so much in love I'm scared the thing will blow up in my face."

He turned on Rick, his dark gaze brooding. "I guess you could add that up to a motive for murder. Is that what you wanted?"

Rick finished his drink and when Ashley reached for it,

he pulled the glass back and shook his head. He could not meet his friend's eyes because he didn't like what he was doing and was, in a sense, ashamed. But neither could he forget the grand jury and the threat of indictment.

"Not quite, Tom," he said and then he was relating the story Nancy had told him, the things she had felt and heard the night Frieda was killed. When there was no reply he spoke of Clyde Eastman's experience.

"I don't know if Eastman is telling the truth," he said, "but he'll have to repeat it officially. He says that while you were supposed to be parked at the shore thinking about a story your car was right out back of this house. You can explain that now or not, as you like," he said. "You don't have to tell me anything, Tom, but I can't hold out on the police any longer."

He spoke of Frederick Brainard's pressure on the state's attorney and what Bob Johnson had told him about the grand jury.

"You know how it looks to me, don't you? You phoned me that afternoon and I told you when Frieda was coming. You knew where she'd be around nine o'clock. I think you sat here in the dark after you'd put the car out back. You didn't want anyone to know you were home but you were going to wait for Frieda to leave my place. You were going to have it out with her. I don't say you planned to kill her but you must have had something in mind."

Ashley knocked the dottle from his pipe and blew through the stem. He tapped it absently against his teeth before he put the pipe aside. He picked up his glass and now his rugged face was grave and shiny in the lamplight.

"I washed the car late that afternoon," he said quietly. "I washed it out back because it was shady there. Afterwards I sat here thinking. I made a drink and then another and then I went out to eat."

He paused, his gaze remote. "When I came back it was about eight thirty and I can't tell you why I put the car out back again because I don't know. Maybe I wasn't thinking and just put it back where I got it; maybe I had something else in mind and did it on purpose. It was dark then and I came in and got a brandy and then another and all the time I was wondering what I was going to do. I saw the lights in your place and finally I went over there. I guess I must have had some thought about seeing Frieda or I wouldn't have gone. Anyway, I did. I'm not sure what time it was and I didn't know what had happened, so I walked round and looked in your window. Frieda was on the floor and I couldn't see you or anyone else. I went inside."

He reached over to open a desk drawer. From the back of it he withdrew some glistening yellow object and turned it over in his big hand before he tossed it lightly to Rick.

Apparently a gold cigarette lighter, it was about two inches square and a quarter of an inch thick, heavy for its size, the surface engine-turned except for a small rectangle on which had been engraved the figures 8-9-56.

"Her bag had been knocked open," Ashley said. "Stuff spilled all over the floor. This was under the davenport. Standing up you probably wouldn't see it but I was hunkered down beside Frieda, knowing she was dead. I was too shocked to do much thinking but I saw this thing and reached for it, not knowing what it was. I was still there when I heard the car stop out front."

He paused to rub one hand hard across his brow. "I didn't know who it was. All I knew was I had to get out of there. I didn't even know I still had that thing in my hand until I was halfway home. I don't know why I stopped in the kitchen either, but I did. I heard someone come in and then a cry, a woman's cry. I started to leave but I was shaking pretty bad and maybe that's why Nancy heard me at the door. I took off across the field and got into my car and beat it with the lights off until I thought I was safe."

Rick remembered the open bag, the spilled contents on the rug. He could see the picture clearly and understood how the lighter could have skidded under the divan. But— His head came up, his eyes half-closed. There had been another cigarette lighter near the bag. He was positive of this. He said so now.

"She had a lighter. I saw it."

"That's not a lighter," Ashley said. "Flip up the top."

Rick did so and then he saw the little plunger.

"It's a perfume atomizer, or whatever you call 'em. You press that gadget and it squirts perfume. Try it."

Rick found that this was true and the scent was so strong he flipped the top back and closed his finger around it. He knew somehow that this was the end of the story. How much of it was true he could not tell but he also knew it was not for him to judge. He hoisted himself wearily from the chair.

"Okay, Tom. I'm sorry I had to come but I wanted you to know how it was with me. I've got to tell the police in the morning. I haven't any choice."

Nothing moved in Ashley's body or in his face. His dark eyes looked tired but Rick could see no resentment in them and somehow that made him feel worse.

"Sure, Rick." Ashley lifted one shoulder an inch and let it drop. "I can't say I blame you. . . . Thanks for warning me, anyway," he said. "I guess you know your way out."

Rick wanted to say something else but the words would not come, so he turned into the hall and felt his way out through the doorway into the night.

16

BY THE TIME Rick Sheridan was back in his own house it seemed to him that he had never felt worse in his life. He wanted a drink but refused to give in to the desire. He knew the gnawing emptiness inside him did not come from hunger but he went into the kitchen with the hope that something in his stomach might help to settle it.

There was about a cup of milk in the refrigerator and an oblong of stale cheese and when he had carved off a small piece he poured the milk and found some crackers. Taking two of these, he went into the bedroom, chewing as he moved and using the milk to help him swallow.

He sat on the edge of the bed but he lacked the energy to start undressing. What he was unable to do was to stop thinking and presently a detail occurred to him that he had forgotten. Neither he nor Ashley had mentioned it and he began to wonder what the explanation was.

"If Ashley had killed Frieda, what happened to her car?"

This was what he asked himself and now he began to speculate about the time element. Suppose Ashley had been waiting outside when he, Rick, had stormed from the house. Suppose he had come inside and found Frieda in her fury. In such a mood she could aggravate any man, particularly one whose happiness and future she had threatened.

If Ashley had killed her it would not have taken long. In a panic then, wanting to make it look as if someone not in the neighborhood was guilty, he would have to get rid of the car.

A man who knew the roads and was a good driver might make the South Norwalk station in ten minutes at that time of night. A couple of minutes to find a taxi, another ten minutes to ride to some point not too far from her. Another two or three minutes to run cross country to his place—

129

But he had not done that. He had come back here. To make sure he had left nothing that would point to him?

How long would that have taken?

With the breaks, twenty-five minutes. Give him thirty and say he had left here at ten or twelve minutes after nine and he still could have made it before Nancy drove up. . . .

He finished his milk and lit a cigarette. Absently he untied his shoes and kicked them off. He got out of his shirt and still he sat there because there was one point he could not be sure of.

The gold atomizer.

Ashley might have taken this just as he said he had, not knowing he was doing it when he heard Nancy coming. But if this was so, why should he have handed over that atomizer tonight?

Somewhere in the distance an automobile horn beeped and was still. Rick sat where he was, no longer conscious of time, his angular face twisted and the cigarette slanting from his lips while the question went round and round inside his head. It was then that he heard the shots.

Never for an instant did he believe that what he heard might be a car backfiring. He had heard too much gunfire in his life to be fooled this time. Three shots in all—two of them close together, the third a second or two later. *And he knew the direction from which they had come.*

That was what shook him. That was why he reached for his shoes and jammed his bare feet into them, pulling the laces tight but taking no time to tie them.

He was on his feet now, already running as he went through the living room, afraid to think but somehow noticing the clock and realizing that it had been barely twenty minutes since he had left Tom Ashley.

His heart was pounding as he dashed out the front door, not from exertion but from an emotional pressure that fed upon an oddly paralyzing sort of fear. He cut sharply as he hit the lawn and then, as the darkness swallowed him, he was racing down the side of the road, his strides awkward and clumsy as he tried to keep his shoes from falling off. He cursed himself for not tying them but would not stop, and now the headlights of an approaching car projected his lengthening shadow on the road ahead as it came up behind him.

He did not hesitate, but he half turned as the car sped past and now, up ahead, he saw something sprawled by the roadside. For a second or two then the car slowed and swung slightly to one side so that its lights gave more definition to the inert object by the roadside.

Rick yelled at the car in the hope that it would stop. For a moment he thought it would do so and his mind automatically registered the number of the license plate. Then, closer now and still running, he began to curse as he saw the lights angle away and watched the car pick up speed.

The dryness in his throat closed round his words as the light diminished. His helpless curses became whispers but he mentally repeated the license number, remembering everything except the first letter. Blank-A-710. . . . Blank-A-710. . . .

He was sobbing for breath when he reached the edge of Ashley's lawn. He could see the white of the T-shirt against the grass before the man's motionless form took shape, and somehow he had skidded to one knee beside it, aware that Tom Ashley lay on his side, head pillowed on one outstretched arm. One foot was bare, the moccasin beside it, and now Rick called out, his voice husky with fear and exertion.

"Tom . . . *Tom!*"

He reached for a shoulder to shake it. He felt the weight of the torso as it rolled limply on its back. He saw the dark stain on the chest that seemed to widen even as he stared down at it. Finally he found some way to think, to understand that even minutes might be vital.

On his feet even as the thought came to him, he wheeled and headed for the front door. Then he was in the study and grabbing for the telephone and almost losing it because his palms were so wet.

He got the operator and said what he had to say about the police and the ambulance. He put the telephone back and stood a moment to look round the familiar room, seeing the pipe Tom had used, the empty glasses with bits of melted ice still standing in the bottoms, the bourbon bottle that was now two-thirds empty.

Somehow he got back out beside the road and this time he leaned close and lifted a bare arm that was heavy in his hand. He slid his fingers along the wrist and pressed hard. He kept them there with breath held. For one brief instant he thought he felt a beat but when he tried again he understood that what he had felt was not the pulsing of Tom's heart but his own.

He put the arm down, the sickness rising in him. He stood up and swallowed against the nausea in his throat. To contain it he put his head back and breathed deeply. No car came by as he stood there and there was no sound in the night.

For perhaps three or four minutes he stood like that and gradually the spasm of his sickness passed. He accepted the fact that his friend he had so recently accused was dead; he also began to think. The helpless rage, the feeling of futility that had gripped him, abated and became a cold and calculating force, and when he again turned toward the house a new purpose was churning in his mind.

He was certain now that this murder could not be coincidence, as it might well have been in Frieda's case. He could not believe that someone just happened to drive up during that twenty minutes after he had left, nor did he think that Ashley had made a date for this particular time.

Instead, someone must have come earlier, perhaps while they were still talking in the study. That someone had parked near by and waited until Ashley was alone before he had come here. There might have been another talk in the study while the killer found out what Ashley knew and realized that his own safety could be guaranteed only by Ashley's silence.

Ashley knew he must talk to the police tomorrow. For some reason he had not told Rick the complete truth but he must have known he would have to do so tomorrow if only to save himself. Still not realizing his own danger he had come out of the house with the killer. Here on the lawn the last words—had there been an argument or threats?—had been spoken in the dark and only then, when it was too late, had Ashley seen the gun.

Three shots. The killer running for his car to get away before he could be seen. Ashley staggering the few steps in pursuit before he collapsed. . . .

Rick had been moving back into the study as these thoughts came to him and now he picked up the New York telephone directory and found Stuart Gorton's number. Moments later he heard it ringing and he counted each one before he hung up and reached for the local directory.

When he had Clyde Eastman's number he dialed it. Again he counted the distant ringing and once more there was no reply. The third number he knew. He dialed. He listened to the first two rings and then a woman answered, her voice sounding thick with sleep.

"Yes. . . . This is the Farrell residence," she said, as though not quite understanding what Rick had said.

"Elinor? . . . This is Rick Sheridan. I'm sorry to bother you but I wanted to speak to Austin. Is he there?"

"Oh—Rick? Why, no, he isn't. But I'm expecting him. He said he would be staying in the city for dinner. He should be here any time now. Shall I have him—"

"No. . . . No, that's all right. I'll try in the morning, Elinor."

Well, he thought bitterly, *that's that. No alibis for anyone.*

He put the telephone down and stood up. As he did so he heard a car skid to a stop outside, and that told him the state police were here. Aware that his time was up, he took another breath and went outside to meet the early arrivals.

The routine that followed was somewhat more familiar this time. There were the usual cars, the same specialists, the air of businesslike confusion which eventually took on a pattern of its own.

As before, Lieutenant Legett was the first officer of rank on the scene and after he had been given a brief fill-in he said Rick could wait in the study—after the bottle, glasses, and ice bucket had been removed for further inspection. A uniformed man remained near the doorway to glance in and see how Rick was doing from time to time but there was no more talk until County Detective Manning came in with the lieutenant.

Manning took his hat off and wiped his brow. This done he began to polish the metal-rimmed glasses. Without them his eyes seemed to take on an added shrewdness.

"You told the lieutenant you left here about twenty minutes before you heard the shots," he said.

"About that."

"How long were you here?"

"I don't know. Maybe a half hour, maybe longer."

"What did you talk about?"

"I thought he might have killed my wife. I told him why I thought so."

"You didn't say anything about that this morning."

"There were a lot of things I didn't know this morning."

"Like what?"

Legett interrupted. "Why don't you start at the beginning, Mr. Sheridan. Try to keep what you said and what he said as close as you can."

Rick folded his bare arms across his undershirt, took a breath and started. It took him quite a while but he got it out in the end. The only thing he missed was the bit about the gold atomizer and something he did not understand made him conveniently forget that part. When he finished Manning swore softly.

"It's happened before," he said irritably. "Instead of coming clean with us so we can handle the job, some people hold out for one reason or another. They can't get it through their thick heads that someone who has killed before may try again when he's cornered. . . . Even that girl friend of yours held out on us about hearing a noise in the kitchen the other night," he snapped.

"She didn't hold out," Rick said. "She was still scared when you questioned her. She forgot it. She didn't even remember to tell me until this afternoon. . . . Did you talk to Clyde Eastman?"

"We haven't located him yet," Legett said.

"Ashley lied about the time," Manning said. "He didn't go over to your house that night when he told you he did," he said to Rick. "He must have gone over there earlier and seen enough to know who did the job. All he had to do was say so and he'd be alive right now."

He growled under his breath and said: "Two shots in the chest. Pretty close up."

"There were three shots," Rick said.

"So you say. There are two slugs in him; that's all we know for sure."

"There were powder burns on his hand," Legett said. "As if he tried to grab the gun. Maybe on the second shot, maybe on the third—if there was a third."

Rick had been watching Manning and now he spoke off the top of his mind. "You'd better tell your boss to call off the grand jury."

Manning tipped his head. He looked at Rick with one eye and then with both. "You knew about that, huh? So why should he call it off?"

"Because no matter what you think about my wife, you

can't tag me for this one. I was home when I heard the shots."

"It would help if you could prove it."

"But I told you," Rick began, not aware that he was shouting and red in the face until Manning cut him off.

"Take it easy, Mr. Sheridan. We're not wearing hearing aids."

Rick swallowed his resentment and tried again. "A car came up behind me just as I ran out of the house. Whoever was in it saw Tom lying there. I thought it was going to stop." He glared at Legett. "I gave you the three numbers and one of the two letters. -A-710. There are only twenty-six letters that could come before the A."

His voice was rising again, not so much from anger as from the lingering shock that had come from finding Ashley's body and the accompanying tension that had become almost too much to bear.

"Find the car and see if I'm not telling the truth," he said. "You want to get the killer, don't you? You don't get a bonus or something for pinning this on me, do you?"

"Bonus?" Legett's reaction was immediate. His mouth tightened and his eyes were cold and hostile. "Who's going to pay us this bonus? . . . Mr. Brainard?"

The blunt rebuttal made Rick realize that his reactions had bordered on the edge of hysteria. He got himself in hand.

"Sorry, Lieutenant," he said stiffly. "I didn't mean that the way it sounded."

Manning was unimpressed. "We'll find the car," he said. "But even if you're right about this it don't have to follow that Ashley and your wife were killed by the same guy. The odds say yes, and they're big odds, but you run into funny things in this business."

He stood up and put on his hat. "We'd better get along and take some more statements. We can stop at your place while you get the rest of your clothes. If you want a drink you can get it then; it may be your last chance for a while."

When they went outside the ambulance had gone. Headlights from two cars sprayed the roadway and lawn and three uniformed men with flashlights were making a minute inspection of the immediate area.

17

THE SESSION with Manning, Legett, and assorted assistants was similar to the one Rick had experienced on Monday night but less protracted. He was home and in bed by three and this time he fell asleep instantly. It was not until he was having coffee at nine thirty the next morning that he came up with a plan of action and knew what he wanted to do.

Heretofore he had been running scared. He had been concerned only with his own problems while unnamed fears pursued him and drove him on. The constant threat of indictment and arrest for a murder he did not commit hovered over him like a bad dream from which there was no solution but complete vindication, not only for himself but for Nancy and his son.

The need for this vindication remained but the threat of indictment had faded somewhat and his own self-interest was mitigated by his thoughts of Tom Ashley. Ashley had made a mistake but his death was cold-blooded and deliberate. Rick could not get the awful picture from his mind and it seemed now that he had a twofold purpose in running down the guilty one. Ashley had given him the gold atomizer and it finally occurred to him that it was this that the two detectives, Deegan and Lynch, had been after when they searched his apartment and house.

He did not know why, but he understood that he needed help badly and now he thought of Sam Crombie. When he had talked to the detective and made an appointment with him at a small restaurant he knew on East Fifty-Third Street, he telephoned Nancy to tell her what had happened the night before. After nearly ten minutes of discussion and argument he gave in to her insistence that she also be allowed to join them.

Rick was the first to arrive and at a quarter of twelve the restaurant was quiet. The hat-check woman had not put in an appearance, the waiters were moving efficiently

136

about the dining room to make sure everything was in order, and the bartender looked a little surprised when Rick slid up on a stool. Not wanting a drink, he orderd a bottle of beer and had just begun to sip it when Nancy came in.

She wore a tailored, tropical-worsted suit that was basically beige and her blond head was bare. She looked very smart and efficient and, to Rick, very lovely. Only the green eyes showed concern as she took the stool next to him and slide her hand along the front of the bar until it found his. She took time to study his face in some effort to assess his mood before she squeezed his hand and spoke.

"You poor darling."

"I'm all right, baby," Rick said. "I'm not so scared any more. I'm just mad."

The barman, who had been watching them, leaned forward. "Can I get you anything, miss?"

"I don't want a drink," Nancy said. "But—a ginger ale might be nice."

The barman went away and the outer door opened again and this time it was Crombie, who doffed his Panama and came puffing to the bar. He asked if he was late and Rick said no.

"Let's get a table," he said. "Do you want a drink?"

Crombie said no and they took their glasses to a table in the corner. Nancy said she wasn't hungry but Rick said they had to eat sometime so how about a sandwich? When they had given their order, he put the atomizer in the center of the table.

Nancy picked it up. She snapped up the top and gave a tentative squeeze to the plunger. Then she gave three or four small sniffs.

"Mean anything to you?" Rick asked.

"Only that the perfume is expensive," she said and passed the atomizer to the detective.

Crombie closed the top and turned it over in his big hand and now Rick was telling his story and explaining where Tom Ashley had found it.

"I saw the bag and the things on the floor," Nancy said, "but I didn't see—" She stopped as the answer came to her. "Oh! But I couldn't have, could I? Tom had been there first."

"You got any ideas, Mr. Sheridan?" Crombie said. "About who might have given this to your wife?"

"One," Rick said and spoke his thoughts about Deegan and Lynch. "Austin Farrell hired them for something. It could have been to look for this."

"Why?"

"The police could trace it, couldn't they? If they found out Farrell had given it to her they'd ask a lot of questions. A thing like this must be pretty expensive. It might be hard to explain."

Crombie nodded to show that he approved of Rick's reasoning. "And the date? 8-9-56 . . . August 9, 1956. Mean anything? Not your wife's birthday, is it?"

"No."

"Maybe it's some anniversary," Nancy said.

"Could be." Crombie leaned forward, his gray eyes busy and one brow warped. "But not necessarily an anniversary we'd think important. A man who's in love with a woman doesn't need much of an excuse to give her a present. He can think of a dozen reasons. Like maybe that date's the anniversary of the first time he met her, or the first time they went out together, or the first time for anything. If he wants to give something he'll find a nice way of doing it."

Rick, watching the broad face, was again impressed by the big man's understanding. So was Nancy. Her young mouth curved in a smile and her voice was soft.

"You must have been in love yourself once, Mr. Crombie."

"Call me Sam," Crombie said and grinned. "Yeah," he said. "Still am, Miss Heath. For thirty-one years. And to the same girl."

"So let's forget the date," Rick said.

"Right," Crombie said. "What we want first is to know who bought it. It looks like solid gold to me and if it is it shouldn't be too hard to trace. Not too many jewelry stores would stock a thing like this. I'll get at it as soon as I leave. Where'll you be later this afternoon?"

"At my apartment," Rick said. "I have to see my agent and after Farrell gets back from lunch I'm going to see him."

"What about me?" Nancy said.

"You go back to work like a good girl," Rick said. "And when you think of it, cross your fingers."

Austin Farrell's offices were in a modest-sized building in the forties that stood between Madison and Fifth. The layout was a little plush for the amount of business he did, but it was the sort of background that Farrell wanted, and his staff included a bright young woman who, it was said, did most of the work; a secretary, a bookkeeper, a switchboard operator-mail girl, and an office boy. Farrell, himself, was very comfortable in the private office that had been done by a high-priced decorator.

The carpet was thick and spotless, the broad desk looked expensive, the deeply padded chair the latest thing in office furniture. His leather client's chair had a cushion that was practically pneumatic, there was an air-conditioning unit in one window and a wall full of books behind the desk. A leather-framed photograph of his wife stood near by and on the broad sill of the other window was a silver tea service. For in the Farrell agency there was no afternoon coffee-break; instead tea was served as a ritual every afternoon at four.

It was early for tea when Rick went in but Farrell was cordial enough and impeccable as ever. His long graying hair lay neatly on his well-shaped skull, a half inch of French cuff showed beneath the sleeves of his dark-blue gabardine suit, and his maroon tie had probably been fashioned by Sulka. He showed perfect teeth as he motioned Rick to the leather chair and asked what he could do for him.

"I wanted to talk to you yesterday," Rick said, "but I didn't want to embarrass Elinor. I think she's suffered enough as it is."

"Embarrass her?" Farrell's smile went away. "How?"

"By telling her about you and Frieda and that Eighth Street hide-out."

Farrell blinked but his voice remained as resonant as ever.

"Eighth Street? I'm afraid I—"

"I'm not guessing about this; I know."

He began to explain how he and Sam Crombie had found the shirt and toilet accessories and relayed the description the janitor had given them about his tenant's latest companion. He could see the change come over Farrell's face and as he continued he recalled some of the things he knew about the man.

At Yale Austin Farrell had been socially active and he made it a point to cultivate only those classmates who might prove helpful to him in later years. He "heeled" for the *News*, and the job he finally got was good enough to get him into a senior society. He had been trading on this ever since and whenever he was out of work he hung around the Yale Club until he had another offer.

Not that he did not offer something in return. He had the personality of an actor bucking for an important part and his manners were the delight of all women, regardless of age. He danced beautifully, he was a considerate escort, and by remaining a bachelor for so many years he was in constant demand as an odd man.

He had worked first for a book publisher as a reader and from there he had caught on with a general circulation magazine as an assistant editor. He had spent the war doing publicity as a Navy officer, most of the time in Washington, and after his discharge he had spent a couple of years as a writer for one of the news magazines. He had come into the agency business as a junior partner of a man named Tate, who for many years had run the small but respected office. For a while the agency was called Tate & Farrell, but soon after he had married and learned that money would no longer be a problem so long as he behaved himself, he bought out Tate, who was at the point of retiring and was glad to take the step.

"I don't get it," Farrell said when Rick had finished. "What is this, some sort of blackmail?"

"Do you deny having an affair with Frieda? Because if you do, let's run down and see if the janitor remembers you."

Farrell compressed his lips and his gaze was both frustrated and resentful. Finally he chose to ignore Rick's suggestion.

"I don't deny that I saw quite a lot of her," he said. "You might say there was a little mutual infatuation but we both understood it was only temporary."

"Maybe Frieda didn't understand it that way. She had one of those mutual-infatuation arrangements with Tom Ashley once. Do you know what happened?"

He waited and when Farrell made no reply he said: "I think Frieda had a tiny streak of cruelty in her that was usually pretty deep down and seldom showed. I don't mean in a physical sense and I think it was something that only developed in the past few years. She was so concerned with her own self-importance—perhaps a little afraid that she would lose it—that when someone hurt her or threatened this illusion she had created and fed on, she struck back with any weapon she could get her hands on."

He spoke of the things Ashley had told him and the threats Frieda had made. "When Tom walked out on her she never forgave him. She threatened to break up his engagement unless she got his next book and I have an idea that under the same circumstances she might have threatened to go to Elinor and quote times and places and chapter and verse. I say, to a guy like you, that could be one hell of a threat."

Farrell had his hands on the desk and suddenly his face was mean and his mouth twisted. He lifted himself two inches out of the chair.

"Just what do you mean, a guy like me? Watch yourself, Sheridan, or I'll toss you out of here on the back of your neck, and don't think I can't do it."

Rick eyed him steadily. He waited until Farrell let his weight back down in the chair.

"You can try if you want to," he said, "but why kid yourself about what I mean? Do you make enough out of this business to live the way you live? All I'm saying is that money is important to you. You've got a rich wife. Behave yourself and you keep her. From what I hear she's going to die long before you do because of her injuries and when she does you'll be fixed. Or am I wrong?"

Rick did not raise his voice or lose his temper but he spoke with a curt succinctness that held attention. He was not impressed by Farrell's display of wrath and the man seemed to know this. He leaned back, his lip twisting with disdain.

"No, you're not wrong," he said. "But I'll tell you something—not that I have to but just to set you straight. I'm devoted to Elinor and if you ask her I think she'll agree. More than ever since the accident. It wasn't my fault but I was driving and I'm not likely to forget it."

He reached into an inlaid, oriental box and removed a cigarette. He tapped it on his thumbnail before he continued.

"But Elinor happens to be a pretty understanding woman. She doesn't expect me to live like a monk. She knows I'm out with some woman now and then. What the hell, have you been one hundred per cent pure since Frieda left you?"

Rick watched flame flare from the gold desk-lighter. He watched Farrell inhale and snap out the flame.

"As a matter of fact I have, but not because my conscience would bother me any. Let's just say I didn't get a proper invitation from a woman I happened to like."

Austin paid little attention to the explanation. He examined his cigarette and said: "The only thing I had to do was be discreet about it—"

"That's exactly my point," Rick cut in. "You might have been discreet with Frieda but it went too far and you couldn't get out. Frieda wouldn't worry about being discreet once you walked out on her. She could be a pretty impetuous mistress; the kind who would make damn sure that Elinor knew the score."

"To stop Frieda, I killed her. Is that what you're getting at?"

"I'm going to prove it if I can."

Farrell laughed aloud, a harsh contemptuous sound. "That'll take some doing. What have you got besides your theory about Frieda?"

"For one thing I know you hired a couple of private detectives named Deegan and Lynch and I think I know why. Before the day's out I'll be sure."

Farrell's glance wavered and he no longer seemed so cocky. He wet his lips and ground out his cigarette.

"Go ahead," he said. "Then start working on my alibi. Elinor and I had dinner at home that night. We were together all evening."

Rick could not argue the point. He did understand that if Elinor loved her husband enough she might lie for him.

"You know about Tom Ashley?"

"I read about it," Farrell said.

"Well, I called Elinor less than fifteen minutes after Tom was shot. She said you weren't home. You were staying in town and she expected you any minute but you hadn't arrived. Where were you?"

Austin pushed back his chair, his glance evasive. "I can prove where I was if I have to," he said, but to Rick it seemed there was more bluster in the tone than conviction.

"Okay," he said as he stood up. "You're going to have to do just that before you're through. . . . I'll see you later, Austin."

18

ONCE Rick Sheridan was back in his apartment he had a hard time to keep from calling Sam Crombie. He knew the detective would get in touch with him as soon as he had some information and to occupy his mind he went over the things he had learned from Farrell.

From there it was easy to go back to the night before, to remember his talk with Tom Ashley, to hear in fancy the three shots, and to live again those horrible moments when he raced down the road in the darkness. That brought him to the car that had passed him and now he went to the telephone and put in a person-to-person call to Manning. The operator had to try twice and when she finally reached the county detective, Rick asked if the police had found the car with the license number -A-710.

For a second or so there was nothing but silence. Then Manning cleared his throat. "Sure we found it. I told you we would, didn't I?"

"Well, what did the driver say?"

"He said he saw you running down the road."

"Didn't he see Ashley?"

"He said he saw a man lying by the side of the road."

"Then why didn't he stop?"

"He was eighteen years old and he had a girl with him that wasn't supposed to be with him. He said he was afraid he'd get her in trouble."

"So," Rick said, feeling a sense of relief but no great elation. "That checks me out, doesn't it?"

"You can still be figured. Let's just say it helps. It looks a lot better than it did."

"You're a pretty stubborn guy."

"In this business you have to be stubborn, if that's the word for it."

Rick started to hang up and then he thought of something else. "Do you know what kind of a gun was used?"

143

"Looks like a .25 calibre."

"Did you find the shells?"

"Does there have to be shells?"

"I never heard of a .25 calibre revolver, did you?"

He could hear Manning's sigh over the telephone before the detective said: "Not yet. . . . You going to be out this way later?"

"Yes."

"I may be seeing you," Manning said. "Keep out of trouble."

When he hung up Rick went into the kitchen and got a can of beer. He brought it to the chair by the window and began to think again. Before long he had a new focal point and slowly the idea that had been no more than a seed of thought began to send out shoots.

Bits of information, many of them half forgotten, seemed now to take on new significance. These led in turn to other facts, and presently he had a pattern that seemed to fit those facts and also to lend new perspective to the over-all picture. He was still busy with his mental exercise and finding a quiet excitement in his progress when the telephone rang.

"Mr. Sheridan?" Sam Crombie said. "We got a line on that atomizer. It was bought three days before the date that was engraved on it at Asbury's on Fifth."

"By whom?"

"Ahh," said Crombie and chuckled. "That's something else again. Asbury's is a pretty high-class shop and very, very discreet. Daddies go in there sometimes and buy platinum-and-diamond trinkets for dolls not always their wives. Asbury's could lose a lot of trade if they gave out information like that."

"Oh." Rick swallowed his disappointment. "Then it doesn't help much, does it?"

"With the police it would be different—and you're going to have to turn this thing over to them pretty soon or you may be in worse trouble."

"I know it," Rick said.

"The police can get the facts from Asbury's but the best I could do is this—and it wasn't easy: The atomizer was bought for cash."

"That figures for Farrell. If he gave it as a present he wouldn't dare charge it because his wife's business manager might mention it and she might ask some questions. All right, hang on to it."

"Until tomorrow," Crombie said. "I got a license to worry about. Tomorrow it's all yours, Mr. Sheridan, and I'm not sure you should wait that long."

"All right," Rick said. "I think I might have a lead now. If it doesn't work the police can have it."

He hung up and went back to his beer. He was just finishing it when someone knocked and he opened the door to find Nancy Heath standing in the hall, a wistful, half-apologetic expression on her young face. She looked about sixteen and she spoke before he could voice his surprise, her voice small.

"Please don't scold me."

Seeing her there so close to him nearly broke him up and he was defenseless against the look in those wide green eyes. It was a very wonderful feeling even though it shocked him a little to find her here.

"Nancy," he said, mustering what disapproval he could. "You know you ought not to come here now."

She hung her head a little and moved up so that he had to step aside. He turned and walked back to the center of the room, not knowing what to say and still disconcerted by her boldness. He heard her close the door before she said:

"I couldn't work. And it's so hot, and I had to find out about the atomizer and what you said to Austin Farrell." She was silent a moment. "I guess I shouldn't have come," she said, sounding so forlorn that Rick was afraid to look at her.

"No, you shouldn't have."

"You men it's not proper."

"Well, it isn't."

More silence.

"Are you driving to the country later?"

"Yes."

"May I go with you?"

"No."

Rick picked up the beer can and found it empty. He put it down hard and walked over to the window, his back turned. He was weakening fast and he knew it. The following silence made it worse. Finally he heard her move and now he felt the touch of her hand on his arm.

"I want to be with you, Rick."

Oh, Lord, he thought. *And how I want to be with you, baby.* But he clung to his remaining resistance as best he could.

"I'm sorry, Nancy," he said. "Even if you did ride out you'd have to come back by train."

"Oh, I wouldn't mind," she said, eagerly seizing this small opening. "Really."

"No."

"Even if I promise to do just what you say? All you have to do is drive by the station. Any station."

Rick was licked and he knew it. He had to look at her and then he had a hard time keeping his hands off her. His grin came grudgingly and once the spell was broken he could speak with mock severity.

"Well, maybe," he said. "If you sit down and stay quiet."

"Oh, I will." She ventured a smile. "I will, Rick."

Her submissiveness was so obviously part of the performance that he started to chuckle. "Do you want a beer? There isn't anything soft around."

"I'm fine," she said and folded her hands in her lap. "You just go ahead and do whatever it was you were doing."

"All right, all right," he said. "You can go. Stop looking so abused. . . . I've got a couple of calls to make," he said and took out his wallet to get the number of Bob Johnson, the lawyer in Bridgeport.

When he had his man he asked if Johnson could get some information from the medical examiner. Johnson said he thought so and Rick told him he wanted to find out if the inside of his wife's mouth had been cut. Then, because he already had a plan of action, he gave the lawyer a telephone number and told him when to call.

His second call was to a reporter he knew who worked on the *Morning Bulletin*. He asked if his friend could look up something for him in the paper's morgue and when the man said yes Rick left his number and said he would wait.

He hung up and looked at Nancy, who seemed not to have moved. "Are you sure you don't want a beer?"

"I'm fine, Rick."

He took his empty can into the kitchen; then went to the bathroom to wash, and comb his hair. The face that looked back at him from the mirror seemed longer and bonier than ever. There was no humor in the steady eyes but there were shadows beneath them put there by strain and weariness. By the time he had pulled his tie to attention and buttoned down the collar points the phone rang. The information that came to him helped to fit one more piece into the puzzle which had begun to take shape in his mind.

19

WHEN Rick Sheridan turned off the parkway at Greenwich, Nancy stirred beside him and gave him a sidewise glance.

"Is this a new way home?"

"No," Rick said. "I have a stop to make."

She did not question him until, ten minutes later, he slowed down on a macadam road close to the Sound. A high stone fence helped to shield the adjoining property from the curious who drove past, but the opening for the driveway showed a broad expanse of carefully tended lawn, a brick Tudor-type house, and another acre of lawn in front that ended in a sea wall. Beyond was a jetty, a diving float and, still farther out, a sleek white sloop that tugged gently at its mooring.

"My," said Nancy when Rick stopped the car beyond the driveway so it could not be seen from the house. "Who lives here?"

"My father-in-law."

"Mr. Brainard? But can't you just drive in and—"

"Not with you, honey. There's no sense in giving him one more excuse to hate me."

"Oh, of course." She leaned back against the seat. "Will you be long?"

"I doubt it."

Rick walked back to the opening in the wall and then he was moving along the curving driveway. The graveled surface was so immaculate it reminded him of a posh golf course where attendants stood by ready to rake the sand traps after they had been used, and when he saw his footprints he stepped to the grassy edge.

An elderly man in an alpaca jacket opened the heavy, arched door in response to his ring. He said good afternoon when he recognized Rick and admitted that Frederick Brainard had just returned from the factory. He said Brainard was on the front veranda and Rick said he could find his way and now he moved down the paneled hall, past the broad staircase, and out on the stone porch that fronted the house.

Brainard was seated in a cushioned canvas chair. He had his jacket off and a cigar in one hand. The small glass-topped table beside him held a tray with a bottle, glasses, a siphon of soda, a bowl of ice, and a plate of tiny sandwiches. He glanced round when he heard Rick but nothing changed in his ruddy face and beneath the bushy brows the dark eyes were bleak.

Rick said he was sorry to barge in like this but there were some things he wanted to get straight. This brought no response, and when Brainard neither asked him to sit down nor offered a drink he knew the going would be tough. He backed to the stone railing and slid one thigh on top.

"Do you still think I killed Frieda?"

"Is that what you came to talk about?"

"Indirectly, yes."

"I'd rather not discuss it with you."

"But I want to discuss it with you," Rick said flatly. "I've found out some things the past couple of days. I've had the help of a good private detective and some of his men because, believe it or not, I'm just as anxious to find out who killed Frieda as you are, but not for the same reason. I'm not interested in revenge."

"Oh," said Brainard with heavy irony. "With you it's just a matter of justice, is that it?"

"Not even that. My reasons are selfish. Unless this business is cleaned up there will always be some doubt. Some people will remember and ask themselves questions. For myself I could take it if I had to but it's no good for the woman I intend to marry when I can; especially it's no good for Ricky.

"I know what you think about me and I've survived your dislike for fourteen years. What you think of me is unimportant and what I think of you is even less important, but so long as you have this idea about my possible guilt in the back of that stubborn, unforgiving mind of yours I'm afraid you'll start contaminating Ricky when you get the chance."

Brainard leaned forward and his eyes flared. "Watch yourself," he said with quiet fury. "I don't have to take that kind of talk from you. I love Ricky just as much as you do."

"I know you do," Rick said. "You'd like nothing better than to have complete custody so you could bring him up the way you want to. And if there could ever be any friendliness or understanding between us I'd like him to visit you now and then, if only because you have so much more to offer in some ways"—he swept one arm to indicate the house and grounds and the private beach and the sloop—"than I have. A boy should love his grandfather and—"

He broke off suddenly because the thoughts of his son were making him emotional and he knew this was not the time to show how deeply he felt his own inadequacy.

"I'm sorry," he said. "I didn't mean to digress and I don't want to get personal. . . . Did you hear what happened to Tom Ashley? Do you think I killed him, too?"

"I didn't even know Ashley. I'm not concerned about whether you did or didn't."

"All right," Rick said, "but there's one thing you should remember. When we find out who did kill Frieda there's going to be a trial. The defense is going to bring up some things about Frieda that you may not know about."

"Like what?"

"I'd rather not say. All I know is that there'll be plenty of publicity. What Frieda has done will be common knowledge. You're not going to like it but you can take it. But what about Ricky? What does a boy of twelve feel about his mother, even one who never gave him much time? What illusions does he have and what does it take to destroy them?"

Brainard was still leaning forward, a look of puzzlement in his dark gaze.

"What the devil are you trying to prove?"

The question brought Rick's thoughts to a stop and he realized that he had digressed again because of his concern for his son.

"I don't know," he said frankly. "That's not what I came to talk about. I came to tell you that I've got an idea who killed Frieda and I'm going to try to—"

"If you've got proof why don't you go to the police?"

"Because I don't have proof. That's just the point. I hope to get it this evening if I'm lucky and if my hunch is right. I stopped to tell you, you can come with me if you want to."

"Why should I?"

"That's for you to decide. If I'm wrong it may be

embarrassing. If I'm right it might be good to have a witness along. After that it will be up to the police. Do you know where the Austin Farrells live?"

"I know Elinor Farrell. I know *about* where they live. I could find it."

"Be there at a quarter of nine."

Frederick Brainard was not used to taking orders. He blinked and bunched his lips and made noises in his throat. Rick slid off the railing and straightened his jacket.

"Not as any favor to me," he said. "But for your own satisfaction. If you'd rather stay here, that's up to you."

He made a small bow and, before Brainard could think of a reply, he walked somewhat stiffly to the front door and disappeared inside.

When Rick Sheridan rolled his car into the parking plaza at the Stamford station he had to stop some distance away. The miniature timetable which all commuters carry told him there would not be a New York train for twenty-five minutes, so he asked Nancy to wait and went in search of a telephone booth.

Clyde Eastman's home phone did not answer and Rick knew it was too late to catch him at the office, so he went back to sit beside Nancy. She had been very quiet during this last part of their ride and this was one of the reasons he loved her. His own mind was too busy for conversation; he had not wanted to explain his intentions; and he particularly did not want to be cross-examined. Now he said he was sorry he had been such poor company. He said he was grateful for her understanding but that all he could tell her now was that he had an idea who might have killed Frieda and Ashley, that he hoped to get enough evidence to prove it.

"Oh," said Nancy. "You don't think you should go to the police?"

"Not yet. And not because I like what I'm doing. I don't know what the police have found out today or what they think. They had me figured as the boy who strangled Frieda and they're not going to stop figuring just because I come up with a theory and some alternate possibilities."

"Isn't it a good theory?"

"I think it is but I'm not governed by the rule book. The police have to proceed by the book because if they don't keep it legal the case is likely to blow up in their face when they get to court. What I'm looking for may not be there tomorrow. It may not even be there now but I have to be sure."

"When will you know?"

"Oh—maybe nine thirty."

"Well, do you think maybe I could—"

She gave the words a tentative inflection and something in her voice told Rick what was coming. He grinned at her and stopped her by touching his finger to her lips.

"No."

She made a pout at him. "At least you could let me finish."

"Okay. Finish. You don't want to take this train, is that it?"

She had to smile at his perception and now she said: "I just thought you have to eat somewhere and why couldn't we pick up some cold cuts and I could fix us supper at your place and then when you finish—"

"Nope," he said. "And stop making it so tough for me."

"But I could take a later train."

"I don't know when I'll be through and I'd feel a lot better if I knew you were home in your own apartment."

"Oh, all right," she said with a sigh of resignation. "But you'll phone me just as soon as you can?"

"Oh, course." Rick glanced at his watch. "Maybe we ought to get out on the platform."

He opened the door for her and went round to meet her. "You don't have to come," she said. "I'd rather you didn't. . . . Tell me, do many of your friends use this station?"

"No," he said, unable this time to forecast her thoughts.

"Well, that's good because I've wanted to do this for quite a while and now I'm going to do it."

She had stopped to face him and now as she finished she put her palms on either side of his face, bending his head slightly as she came up on her toes. She gave him a quick but thoroughly impressive kiss and stepped back.

"There," she said. "Good luck, darling, and do be careful."

Then she had turned away to leave him standing there tingling as she headed for the platform, her shoulders straight, the swing of her hips controlled and graceful.

20

IT WAS getting dark when Rick Sheridan pulled his car to a stop beyond the hedge which screened it from the house. He had given some thought to the element of time because he did not want to be poking about in complete darkness and it seemed now that the gathering dusk was sufficient to give him the protection he needed.

When he had cut the ignition he took one final pull on his cigarette before he dropped it out the window. He had been unable to reach Clyde Eastman—he had telephoned once and detoured past Eastman's house on his way here—but that could not be helped. Now, aware that he was as mentally prepared as he could be under the circumstances, he opened the door, stepped to the pavement, and walked back to the driveway that had been cut deeply into the grassy slope and led to the two-car garage.

For some reason he did not want to move in a crouch but he walked swiftly, aware that even with the difference in elevations between drive and lawn the upper part of his body would be visible to anyone who happened to be watching from the windows. He saw that both cars were in place and seconds later he had moved beneath the open overhead doors and knew he no longer could be seen from outside.

The problem that then presented itself was: Which of the cars should he search first? The Continental was Austin Farrell's personal car but he did not always use it. The smaller sedan often served as his taxi to and from the station and on those days the larger car was left for Elinor and the gardener-chauffeur who took her about when Austin was not available. Finally, because his hunch indicated that the Continental was the car he wanted, he opened the wide door and took out the pencil flashlight he had brought.

For if his theory was right, Tom Ashley had been shot, not on his front lawn as he had first suspected but from a car. An automatic pistol had been used, which meant that it was likely some or all of the expended shells had been ejected inside the tonneau. According to Manning these shells had not been found at the roadside or lawn of Ashley's house—unless they had been discovered fairly recently. Whether or not the person who had pulled the trigger had the intelligence to comb the car for those shells was something else again.

Standing on the garage floor and leaning inside the car, he directed his flash on the carpet in front of the rear seat. He went over this inch by inch. He paid particular attention to the crevices at the front and rear as well as the metal strips on the sides. When he found nothing here he moved in and, on his knees now, went over the seat, sliding his fingers well down into the crack where it met the back rest.

He repeated the procedure on the floor of the front part of the car, depending not only on his eyes and the flashlight but his sense of touch. Gradually then a feeling of futility began to work on him and to fend off his discouragement he continued stubbornly.

The high hopes had faded now. This was to have been the starting point from which his theory could be developed. Without something concrete to support his hope he had only bits of information, most of it intangible, on which to make an accusation. In the end it was this stubbornness that finally paid off.

He did not see the hole in the back rest a quarter of an inch above its juncture with the cushion, and it is unlikely anyone else would have seen it unless he had been looking for it. For the small neat pattern of the upholstery that covered the sponge-rubber base had a dark background and the break in that fabric was tiny.

It was the touch of his finger that found that break, and having found it, the finger probed more deeply. The beam of the flashlight revealed little more on the surface but he knew now he had found a hole. He tried to expand it with the tip of his little finger. When the tough resiliency of the rubber blocked him, he reached into the inside pocket of his jacket and removed the thin, ball point pen which someone had given him, a cheap give-away pen with an advertising message printed along its length.

With the end of this he began to probe anew, his weight driving the point deeper. He was not sure how far the pen had penetrated but he knew finally that the point had come up against something that felt hard and metallic.

By adding leverage he was able to move the tip back and forth, to feel the slight scratch of metal on metal. Then, because he could do no more at the moment, he withdrew the pen and remembered again the three shots he had heard the night before.

Two of these had come one on top of the other. The third was delayed. Because Ashley had died hard? Because he had strength and the will to fight back while he could. There were powder burns on his hand and if they had come from the third shot it seemed likely that he had grabbed the muzzle and twisted it violently aside before that third bullet was fired.

He felt his hopes soar as he completed the thought. If the slug was in the seat, and the gun could be found—

"Okay, Rick!"

He stiffened where he stood, his feet on the garage floor, his weight forward on hands that still rested on the seat. He had heard no sound until those words hit him without warning. He had been too busy with his thoughts and with his search to consider the possibility that he had been seen, but there was no doubt in his mind about the voice.

"Back out! Easy now."

Rick did as directed. He straightened and turned slowly and then he saw the little gun in Austin Farrell's hand.

"Elinor saw you from her window," Farrell said. "She wasn't sure who it was, so I thought I'd have a look. If I have to use this you'll be a prowler I failed to recognize in time."

Rick stood stiff-legged and immobile while he fought off the shock of his surprise. Because he did not want to let on how badly he had been shaken he was careful with his voice.

"That would be a stupid thing to do."

"Would it?"

"Because when they dug the bullet out of me they might just compare it with the two they found in Tom Ashley. Then where would you be?"

"It wouldn't do *you* much good then, would it?"

"That's the gun, isn't it?"

Farrell leaned back against the other car. "What were you looking for?"

"Empty shells."

"You're a little late. So were the police when they came poking about this afternoon."

"Three shells?"

"That's right."

Rick considered speaking of the hole in the upholstery and decided against it. That would be for the police to dig out—if he could stay alive until they got on the job.

"That gun isn't going to do you much good in the end, is it, Austin?" he said.

"I don't know." Farrell glanced down at it. When he looked up his handsome face was tight and some new purpose showed in his eyes. "That'll depend on a lot of things. Shut that door, Rick."

He waited until Rick closed the car door. "Now let's go inside. I think we'd better talk things over. Out the side door and in the back way. Just remember I'll be right behind you and if I have to use the gun I'll probably do it, stupid or not. . . . Get moving!"

It was quite dark as they moved out the door and along a breezeway to the rear entrance. The lights were on here and Rick took no notice of his surroundings but did what Farrell told him until they reached the center hall. He knew his way then and walked ahead, hearing Farrell two paces behind him as their steps synchronized.

Elinor Farrell was sitting in the same chair in which he had last seen her. She wore a loose-fitting navy dress which seemed to accent her pale, well-boned face. Again she had a printed scarf in her lap and her right hand moved beneath it while her left lay motionless on the chair arm.

She was looking right at him as he advanced, and all at once he knew what was wrong with his portrait and why he had been dissatisfied with it the other afternoon. For this was not at all the face he had painted; this was not the woman who had sat for him twice weekly during the past month. The strain showed in the features now and he recognized it as such. The face seemed thinner somehow, the mouth tense, and the eyes which had so often reflected the dignity and serenity that characterized this woman were shocked and afraid.

"He was searching the car," Farrell said. "Sit down, Rick. Over here where I can keep an eye on you."

Rick eased down on the divan that had been placed against a refectory table facing the windows. He looked at the woman and then at the gun. When he let his gaze move upward he did not like what he saw in Farrell's thin-lipped face. Not knowing what came next, he decided to wait and let someone else carry the ball. Farrell might have done so—at least he had started to open his mouth—when the silence was broken by the shrill summons of the telephone.

From his sitting position, Rick jumped about two inches as his reflexes responded to the sound. Elinor stiffened slightly in her chair and glanced at her husband.

"Answer it, Austin."

Farrell backed toward the telephone table and picked up the instrument.

"Yes. . . . Who?" His eyes flicked to Rick and his smooth brow was suddenly warped. "Yes. Who's calling?"

He covered the mouthpiece with his hand and spoke to his wife. "A Mr. Johnson. He wants Rick."

"But—how would he know—"

"I told him to call me here," Rick said.

"Then talk to him," the woman said.

Farrell extended the telephone and spoke softly as he stepped aside and leveled the gun.

"And be damned careful what you say, Sheridan. I'm not fooling."

"Hello," Rick said. "Yes, this is Sheridan."

"I got what you wanted from the medical examiner," Johnson said. "No cuts or wounds of any sort inside your wife's mouth. . . . Is that what you wanted? Have you got a new lead on this?"

"I may have." Rick eyed the gun. "Thanks a lot. I'll call you back."

He hung up before Johnson could reply and again Farrell gestured with the gun.

"What did he want?"

"What difference does it make?"

Farrell chewed on the question a moment. "Go back and sit down."

Rick resumed his seat. He stole a glance at his watch. It was exactly eight forty-six and he began to wonder, not if Brainard was going to be late but whether he would come at all. For he needed Brainard now, needed him badly. Once inside, the older man would help make things tough for Farrell because it was his natural bent to make things tough for anyone who gave him an argument.

"What?" he said in response to something Farrell had said.

"I asked why you told Johnson, whoever he is—"

"He's a lawyer."

"—to call you here?"

"Because after I had searched your car I intended to come in and—"

This time the interruption came from the ring of the doorbell and Rick eased back on the cusions and let his breath out slowly while Farrell and his wife again exchanged startled glances.

"Who the devil can that be?" Farrell said.

He swore softly as the ring was repeated.

Elinor had leaned forward, her hands white-knuckled as she squeezed the arms of her chair. Her face was taut and still as she waited for the next ring and presently it came.

"Let it ring," Farrell said savagely. "Maybe whoever it is will go away."

"I don't think so," Rick said.

"What?" Farrell scowled at him.

"That's probably Brainard."

"Brainard? Don't kid me. Why should he—"

"Because I asked him. I asked him to meet me here at a quarter of nine."

Farrell was glaring now but he still had no answer and when the bell continued to ring, steadily now, he swore again and said: "Let it ring, damn it! He can't break in."

"He'll probably go to the police," Rick said.

"Austin!" Elinor sat up in her chair. "You'll have to answer the door. Maybe you can convince him that we're alone. . . . And give me that before you go, please."

She was looking at the gun now and when Farrell hesitated she spoke again with new authority. "Please do as I say, Austin."

Farrell stepped quickly to the chair and she accepted the automatic in her left hand. Then he wheeled and disappeared in the hall.

Rick waited, breathing shallowly now as his nerves began to tighten. He heard the door open and Farrell's voice. Brainard replied and Farrell answered, and now Brainard's voice rose and there was no difficulty hearing what he said.

"What do you mean, he's not here?" he demanded. "His car's out front and he told me to meet him here. . . . Well, make up your mind. Do I come in or find the nearest telephone and call the police?"

Rick had heard that tone of voice so often over the years that he was used to it. Apparently Farrell was not equipped to combat it at the moment because presently steps sounded in the hall and the door slammed and then Brainard was moving into the room where he looked at Rick and then at the woman before he came to a stop. He also saw the gun.

"What's that for?" he snapped.

"I was searching a car when Farrell came up behind me in the garage," Rick said. "He had the gun. That's why I'm sitting here. Thanks for coming."

Brainard did not seem to hear this last. He was watching Farrell, his face stiff and his eyes savage beneath the bushy brows. Normally he was not a profane man and to women of his class he had a certain courtliness. At this moment however the pressure was too much for him to bear.

"So you're the miserable bastard who did it?" he said.

"Mr. Brainard."

Brainard's hands flexed at his sides but something in the woman's tone made him look at her.

"Please sit down," Elinor said.

"Why? This is a matter for the police now, isn't it?" He turned on Rick. "You can prove he did it, can't you?"

"I know some things that may help," Rick said. "If I can get a chance to explain them. When I finish you can decide for yourself."

Brainard thought it over. "All right." He picked out a straight-backed chair and sat down. "Let's get started."

Rick took a second to look at his audience one at a time. This was what he had come for and now he had his chance. The trouble was there were so many things inside his head that crowded for expression he did not know quite how to start. He swallowed and wet his lips. When he was ready he spoke first of Tom Ashley.

He related some of the things Ashley had told him in their last conversation and spoke of his suspicions.

"Tom was at my place somewhere around the time Frieda was killed," he said. "He lied about his movements because we know now he must have known who killed her. Until then he had protected this person. I don't know why except that Frieda was threatening his happiness and her death removed the pressure. I suppose it may have seemed like a favor to him and he was willing to let it go at that."

"Wait a minute!" Brainard spoke harshly. "What's this about Frieda blackmailing him."

Rick told the truth as he knew it and the look in the older man's eyes told him that Brainard had never suspected that his daughter might have had an affair with Ashley or anyone else.

"Whatever the reason," Rick went on, "Tom knew he could not hold out any longer. I had enough facts and theory to cause his arrest in the morning and he knew I intended to go to the police with what I had. . . . The mistake he made was in calling the killer as soon as I left. He was a very decent guy and he must have wanted to explain why he had to tell the truth; when he finished the killer must have begged for a final interview."

He paused and said: "I thought there had been an argument and that Tom had been shot outside in the darkness. I know now it didn't happen that way. . . . I was sitting in my bedroom when I heard those shots and I finally remembered that I had heard an automobile horn a few minutes before that.

"What happened," he said, "is that the killer blew his horn and Tom came out to the car, never dreaming that the person he had protected would turn on him. He was shot down from that car, probably without warning, without a chance. As he staggered back and fell the car moved off. It was out of sight by the time I could run out of the house."

He went on hurriedly to tell what he had done and how he had called the police. "When I knew he was dead I got an idea," he said. "I made three calls. Neither Eastman nor Gorton, who had possible motives for murder, were home, so I called here. From the time I heard the shots until I made this last call was perhaps fifteen minutes—no longer. But it's only a ten-minute drive from Tom's place to here; time enough to get back before the call came. You answered, Elinor."

The woman nodded. "I know."

"You said Austin wasn't here."

"Which was true."

"You had to say that because if I asked to speak to him you would have been trapped. You pretended you'd been asleep but you weren't, were you?"

"What do you mean?"

"When Austin goes in town he usually takes the small car to the station. He was in town last night—and that left the Continental. I say Ashley was shot from that car and I can prove it. I think you drove it. Even with a crippled leg you can drive a car with an automatic shift. I know you can because you drove a car away from my house the night Frieda was strangled."

"What's all this?" Brainard leaned forward and seemed about to spring from the chair. "Elinor? You're saying Elinor killed her? I thought it was Farrell."

"So did I," Rick said, "until after I'd left his office and had a chance to add up a few things. . . . Yes," he said as he let out his breath, "Elinor killed her. Didn't you, Elinor?"

21

THE SILENCE that came with Rick's announcement lasted for three long seconds and was finally broken by Farrell. Until then he had been standing and now he made some small throaty sound that could have been a muffled groan. His shoulders sagged and he moved slowly over to the chair that faced his wife and let himself down wearily.

Brainard remained as he was, his bushy brows bunched over eyes that gradually lost the look of incredulity to narrow fixedly on the woman. Elinor's body remained at ease. The gun lay under her left hand on the arm of the chair and finally she lifted the hand to gesture emptily.

"You can't be serious, Rick." She smiled and it was not a bad effort under the circumstances. "I can't understand why you should accuse me like this when you have nothing to offer but some wild guesses. Surely there must be more than that."

"A couple of things, Elinor," Rick said. "Some of them so minor I might not have remembered them at all if it hadn't been for the atomizer."

"The atomizer?"

"What atomizer?" Brainard said.

Rick described it for him and explained how Tom Ashley had found it and taken it with him without meaning to.

"There was a date on it," he said. "August 9, 1956. Sam Crombie, a detective who is helping me, said the date didn't have to mean much. He said a man in love could find plenty of excuses to give a woman a present and that such a date might be important only to them.

"He checked on the atomizer this afternoon," he said, "and found it came from Asbury's. It was purchased three days before that date—August 6—and paid for in cash. The police can find out who bought it but we had to make our own assumptions. We figured it was Farrell," he said and

162

digressed to speak of the activities of Deegan and Lynch.

"They searched Nancy Heath's apartment. They searched my apartment and house but they took nothing. Crombie and I figured they were after the atomizer and we know they were working for Farrell. We thought the atomizer had spilled out of Frieda's bag and Farrell wanted it so it could not be traced to him. Then I remembered something."

He digressed again to explain how he and Crombie had searched Frieda's apartment the morning after she had been killed.

"There were some carbons of letters she had written to the office when she was abroad. I happened to read one that was written exactly a year before on August 6th."

"The day the atomizer was bought," Brainard said.

"Right," Rick said, "and I couldn't figure why Farrell"— he glanced across the room—"would buy an atomizer for Frieda and have it marked August 9 when he couldn't possibly hope to get it to her in time. She was in Geneva. She was going to Lake Como and Milan and Genoa. It made no sense. What did make some sense was the fact that I was doing a portrait of Elinor that had to be done tomorrow—the 9th—because of a very special occasion."

He looked at the woman. "According to the *Bulletin* you and Austin were married six years ago tomorrow. August 9, 1956 was your fifth wedding anniversary. Austin bought that atomizer for you. He had it marked. He paid in cash because he wanted to give you a present he had paid for himself and not something on a charge account the way he bought almost everything else. . . . That's why you had to have that portrait tomorrow, isn't it, Elinor?"

When she made no reply he turned to Brainard. "They must have learned the police had found no atomizer. They couldn't know Ashley had it, and that left Nancy and me. If either of us had it, or turned it over to the police, it might not be too hard to prove that the atomizer was not Frieda's.

"I tried to get Clyde Eastman before I came," he said to the woman. "I wanted to see if he ever remembered having seen Frieda use such an atomizer, but that can wait. For now I have to assume it belonged to you and the fact that Ashley found it on the floor proves that you were there that night. . . . You must have dropped your bag, too."

She still had not moved and her self-control was quite remarkable. "Is that all you have, Rick? It isn't very much, is it? Because you see, even assuming you are right about it, there could be only one person who could prove the atomizer had ever been on your living room floor. . . . And he's dead."

Rick looked at her in amazement because what she said was so true. Her composure was almost unbelievable, but what bothered him most was the fact that she could think so clearly under pressure. He took a small breath and tried again, the sheen of perspiration coating his angular face and some new dryness in his throat.

"The other day when Nancy and I were here the portrait bothered me. I've always been pretty good on likenesses but it seemed then that I'd missed. It was not the same face I had painted and I didn't know why; neither did Nancy. It didn't occur to me that there was a reason why the nice things I had once seen in your face were no longer there. What I saw was strain and fear and uncertainty and I wasn't smart enough to sense it. But habit is a funny thing, Elinor, and you've always made it a point to be very gracious about shaking hands."

"Oh?"

"Each time you came to my studio and each time you left you shook hands. You did it when you left on Monday afternoon and I thought about it at the time. But on Wednesday afternoon when we came you didn't shake hands with me. You didn't shake hands when I introduced you to Nancy. You gave her your left. You had a scarf in your lap just as you have now and you kept your right hand out of sight.

"That telephone call I got earlier was from a lawyer. The police told me that there was a trace of blood in Frieda's mouth. The lawyer checked with the medical examiner and there was no sign of a cut or wound inside Frieda's mouth. Which means it was not her blood. She fought back when you tried to get her by the throat, didn't she? Where did the blood come from, Elinor? Did she manage to bite your hand?"

As he paused he saw the woman push the scarf aside and raise her right hand. She turned it over and from where he sat there was not much he could see.

"It hardly shows now," she said. "I doubt if the police

could prove very much by that. It was clever of you to think of it, Rick, but it isn't important, is it? And what about the motive? Exactly how did I happen to be at your place Monday night, or was that coincidence too?"

"Look here," said Brainard, who was never a patient man. "Let's stop all this nonsense. I say it's time the police took over and—"

"Please."

It was the same cool, controlled voice that had cut him off before and it stopped him again.

"We're here to talk this over, aren't we? I'd like to hear what else Rick has to say."

She looked back at him and all at once he felt a thrust of resentment where none had been before. Such calculated effrontery rubbed him the wrong way and he suddenly realized that this woman was no longer deserving of any sympathy. She had killed Frieda, probably in a fit of passionate anger rather than with premeditation, but she had shot Ashley down deliberately, and now Rick leaned forward again, his jaw tight and his voice curt.

"All right, Elinor," he said. "I think you knew Austin was having an affair with Frieda and had been for some time." He heard Brainard sputter some unintelligible sound but ignored him. "If I have to guess I'd say you already had Deegan and Lynch working for you. Austin got them in a hurry the morning after the murder, so I say you already knew about them—not that it matters. The point is, you were afraid that this time you'd lose your husband. This was not some attractive number who had been induced to spend the night with him. This was serious.

"Until then you controlled Austin because you had the money and you knew how important it was to him. But Frieda had a nice income and in a few years she'd have the principal. You knew I was in love with Nancy. From other talks we'd had while you were sitting for me you knew Frieda had refused to give me a divorce. But Monday she phoned while you were there. You heard what I said about still wanting the divorce, which could only mean that Frieda had changed her mind and was willing to talk it over."

He turned to Brainard. "You had dinner with her that night. What did she say about a divorce? Are you the one who insisted she ask for custody of Ricky?"

Brainard's troubled gaze held for a moment and then he

glanced down at his hands. He nodded slowly. "Yes," he said.

"But she decided she wanted one anyway, didn't she?"

Again the nod and now Rick continued to Elinor. "In your mind there could only be one reason why Frieda had changed her mind. Did you accuse Austin? Did he deny it?"

He paused and said: "It doesn't matter because deny it or not I say you forced him to drive to my place. There's a little lane just down the road and there was a car in it that night when Nancy let me out in front of the house. You knew Frieda was coming at nine and you were there ahead of time. You didn't expect me to come out after our talk but you knew Frieda would and you were ready to pull up alongside her car and have it out with her one way or another. Instead of that I came out and stormed off down the road. When Frieda didn't come out right away you had Austin drive across the road and help you out of the car while you went in alone."

As he hesitated his mind evolved a picture of what must have happened. He could almost see the woman's movements as she made her labored way with her crutch and crippled leg. Pride made her avoid help when she could and she had gone into the living room to find a furious and thwarted Frieda, who by then had picked herself off the floor and was probably emotionally unable to listen to reason. He knew what Frieda would be like under such circumstances but he saw no point at guessing at details. He said so. He said he did not know what happened then.

"She must have knocked your bag out of your hand," he said, "and it spilled open. That's the only way the atomizer could have skidded under the divan without your knowing it. You picked up your other things—did you have that gun with you then?—and when you left and realized what you had done you made Austin help you. Isn't that the way it happened, Elinor?"

He took a breath. "You had to tell him, didn't you? You had to have help and he could give it or get cut off without a dime. You made him help you into your car. You got the idea of driving Frieda's convertible off to confuse the police. You made Austin follow you to South Norwalk and park it near the station. Then when the police came you could tell them you and Austin were together all evening."

He stopped then because he had run out of words. He reached for a handkerchief to mop his face and dry his wet palms and the woman still sat there unmoved. The mask of her self-control remained intact and if her voice was no longer so steady it reflected no fear.

"You make it sound very convincing, Rick," she said. "I suppose it could have happened that way. . . . But you can't prove it." She paused. "Can you?"

"No," Rick said. "But I can prove you killed Tom Ashley and that should be enough."

For the first time then he saw the uncertainty in her dark-blue eyes. Her lower lip trembled and she caught it with her teeth. When she had mastered the spasm her head came up again.

"Can you really? How, Rick?"

"You were ready with that gun when Tom came out of his house last night. There was no longer any question in your mind about killing him. Whatever he had seen that first night was enough to convict you and he had run out of time. When he stepped up to the lowered window you shot him twice. But he didn't fall, did he?"

He hesitated then to wonder if he should reveal the one clue that would count the most. At first afraid to mention it lest Farrell find some way to destroy or remove the buried bullet, he now decided that with Brainard here to help the odds were at least even in spite of the gun. He saw, too, that his blunt convincing words had begun to undermine the woman's resistance. No longer did the eyes challenge him and there was no color in her cheeks.

"Tom was hit fatally," he said, "but he was still alive. I guess the last thing he did was to grab for that gun—the powder burns on his hand prove that—and twist it aside. That third slug never left the car, Elinor."

Farrell spoke then, a ragged cry that had no meaning for Rick. He did not even look at the man but he heard the woman say:

"I don't believe it. The police—"

"Yes, the police looked," Rick cut in. "But they were looking for the empty shells that Austin had already removed. I didn't see that little hole either. I just happened to feel the tear in the fabric."

Farrell must have been convinced because he came out of his chair, a haggard look on his handsome face and his eyes a little wild.

"I can get it, Elinor."

"You don't know where it is," she said dully.

"I can find it."

"Not now you can't!"

Brainard had opened his jacket. Just where he had kept the gun Rick could not tell but it was in his hand now. He was not looking at Farrell; he was watching the woman and when Rick brought his eyes round he saw that she was holding the little automatic. Brainard must have seen it, too, but it did not seem to bother him.

"Take one step toward that door, Farrell," he said, "and I'll drop you."

"If you do I'll have to shoot, Mr. Brainard."

"That's a chance I'll have to take. You killed my daughter and this time you're going to pay for it."

"Yes." The woman's shoulders moved as she took a deep breath. "I realize that now. But why risk your life when perhaps there is a better way?"

Brainard did not understand her. His expression showed it. He watched her put the gun back on the chair arm, no longer pointing it but covering it with her hand. He glanced from her to her husband and finally his own grip relaxed.

"Go ahead," he said. "I guess a few minutes isn't going to make much difference."

22

IN THE SECOND or two of silence that followed Rick was afraid that Elinor's apparent resignation was but a mask for some trap that would presently come to light. This, he knew, was a calculating mind, the craftiness more pointed because of her desperation but nonetheless a fundamental part of her character. It was only later that he began to understand the reason for her suggestion. What followed was a confession and a plea for a compromise, and she directed her opening remarks at Brainard.

"If you want to know why I killed your daughter I'll tell you, but don't expect any remorse or regret from me. I had as much right to protect what was mine as she had to take it away. If she'd had the good sense to understand that much there would have been no trouble. She was not a nice person, Mr. Brainard, but she wasn't dealing with a man this time, she was dealing with someone who could match her ruthlessness. . . . You see, I had a great deal to lose because I loved my husband and always have."

She took a moment to glance at Farrell and continued to Brainard. "A part of my mind hated him, I suppose, for the accident and what it did to me, and I demanded a certain measure of devotion and attention. It was my price for the money he spent so freely but I knew I could not chain him to my side, nor did I want to. In a way I suppose I was buying his affection, but if that was what I wanted why should it matter to anyone else? He was important, do you understand that? He was the one thing I had left I could count on. Because you see, my condition is getting progressively worse," she said. "Two years from now, if I was still alive, which is questionable, I would be a complete invalid."

In the same quiet tone she said: "A woman can tell when the man she loves changes. I knew something was happening to Austin and because it frightened me I hired those two detectives Rick mentioned. What I learned from

169

them told me Austin was having an affair with Frieda but I was afraid to risk accusing him or issuing any ultimatum because I knew she had money, too, and she was attractive enough and"—her voice broke slightly—"she had a sound and healthy body."

She looked at Rick and went on quickly to cover up that moment of weakness.

"You guessed right about the phone call I overheard," she said. "Until then I had been afraid but I had been protected by the knowledge that Frieda did not want a divorce and I was willing to wait for the affair to break up. What you said that afternoon left me in a panic and that night at dinner I told Austin what I knew, didn't I, Austin? And what did you say?"

Farrell had again slumped in his chair, his face slack and his gaze remote.

"I admitted it," he said thickly. "I told you it was true but you were wrong about my wanting to marry her."

"Maybe. I still don't know whether you lied about that or not. I do know she had changed her mind about divorcing Rick and why should she do that unless she thought she could get you?"

She turned back to Rick. "I told Austin we would have it out that night, the three of us. I made him come. I told him if he didn't I not only would cut him off but I would kill Frieda, and I think I meant it. . . . I knew she was due at your place at nine and Austin parked the car in that little lane where you said he did. When Frieda came out I was going to have Austin crowd her to the side of the road. Out there in the country with no one to help her I knew I'd get the truth.

"Only she didn't come out," she said. "You did. So I had Austin drive up beside her car. I made him help me out and I went inside with my crutch and when she saw me she started screaming at me. I don't know what happened between you—"

"She slapped me," Rick said, admitting his shame aloud for the first time, "and I slapped her back and she fell. It was the first time I had ever touched her and that's why I got out. I was afraid of what I might do."

"I didn't know that," Elinor said. "And what we said to each other I will never remember. We simply screamed at each other and I was standing by the divan and she pushed me—hard. I fell back," she said, her voice hardly more than a whisper as her mind re-created the scene.

"But as I went back on the divan I grabbed her wrist and pulled her toward me." She glanced down. "I have a lot of strength in my hands now; even the left one though it is beginning to feel prickly at times. I hung on and twisted her wrist and she went to her knees in front of me.

"That's when she bit me," she said. "She put her teeth in the back of my hand and that infuriated me even more and somehow I had her by the throat with one hand. I jerked the other one free and twisted it in that scarf. I hung on until she was quiet and when I finally let go she slumped down and lay still. . . . That's how it happened. I hadn't planned it that way. I had no plan at all except to protect what was mine."

Rick believed her. It was easy to visualize the step-by-step progression that led to murder and now he sat very still as she continued.

"Nearly everything had spilled from my bag. I didn't see the atomizer but my compact was open and some of the powder had spilled onto the rug. I thought the police might be able to trace it, so after I had picked up my things I opened Frieda's bag so it would look as if it had been dropped that way. I sprinkled a little powder from her compact so it would mix with mine and left it open so the police would think it came from there. I made my way outside. Austin was pacing back and forth. He'd heard us screaming but he'd been afraid to come in—"

"He didn't have to help you," Brainard cut in. "When he found out it was murder he—"

This time she interrupted. "Oh, yes, he did have to help, Mr. Brainard. I told him exactly what I intended to do. I told him I was changing my will in the morning to cut him off. If I was convicted of murder and had to pay the penalty he wouldn't get a penny. If he helped and I could get away with it I would then fix the will so he would inherit everything.

"I never had much doubt about Austin," she said. "Austin has a weakness, Mr. Brainard. All his life he has worshiped material things like fine cars and good clothes, and right clubs and the best restaurants. I think he prizes that good life of his more than anything. When we got home and I missed the atomizer he was already involved too deeply to back out."

Rick cleared his throat as she finished. "Tom Ashley

saw you," he said. "He wanted to see Freida that night, too."

"He saw us drive the cars away. When he went in and found Frieda he knew what must have happened. . . . He came to me the next day and told me what he knew. He did not blame me. I guess he felt sorry for me or—maybe he realized that in a way I had done him a favor. But he was a friend of yours and he said you were in trouble. He said if you were indicted for murder he would have to tell the truth. I had to agree to what he said."

"Yes," Rick said because it was the sort of thing Ashley would do. "And last night he telephoned you as soon as I left. He told you he couldn't hold out any longer, that he would have to tell the police in the morning. You begged for a chance to talk to him again. You must have said you would drive right over."

"Yes."

"With that gun. Knowing exactly what you intended to do."

"Yes, I knew. I made myself look at Ashley not as a person but as a threat that had to be removed. Once you have killed you can never be the same. Your thoughts are not normal thoughts. There is always the fear. With me it was not the fear of my life but the fear of spending what little time I have left in prison or a death cell."

Her left hand picked up the gun and she inspected it with care.

"I have no excuse. I could say that I was temporarily insane—and perhaps I was—but all I know for sure is that I was glad it was dark, that I could not see his face. I pulled the trigger and the gun went off twice and he did not fall. I remember my terror when he grabbed for it before I could fire the third shot. I never knew where it went but I saw him stagger back and start to collapse. I do not remember driving back but if you had called a minute earlier I would not have been here to answer. . . . You were not bluffing about the third bullet, were you, Rick? You really did find it in the car?"

"It's there now," Rick said.

"All right." Brainard stood up, his voice low but savage. "That's enough. I'm phoning the police."

"Wait, Mr. Brainard. There's a better way."

"Oh, no."

"I think there is. If you try to call now I will have to shoot. You may be killed, and Rick, too. That I will also be killed is no threat to me now. Must there be more killing?"

"All you have to do is put down that gun and there won't be any more killing."

"I've told you the truth. The bullet in the car will give the police the proof they need. I'm not asking for sympathy. I have no use for it. But I am still in a position to bargain."

"No bargains," Brainard said.

Rick eased himself off the divan. He watched Brainard back toward the telephone, the gun in his hand leveled. He saw the woman point the little automatic, and spoke quickly as some strange and shapeless fear took hold of him.

"Hold it!" he snapped, wanting only to gain time enough to think. "What do you mean, bargain?"

The woman looked at him. "I want your word that you will not go to the police until morning."

"No," Brainard said.

Farrell was on his feet now, his gaze bright with terror and uncertainty as it flicked from his wife to Brainard and back again.

"Elinor—"

"Be quiet, Austin!"

Farrell appealed to Brainard. "Don't be a fool. What difference does it make to you? You've got what you wanted." He took a tortured breath. "She means it. Can't you see that?"

"Until midnight then, Mr. Brainard," Elinor said. "Give me your word—"

"So you can swallow a handful of sleeping pills and take the easy way out? No, by God! You killed my daughter and you're going to pay for it just like any other murderer."

He was reaching behind him for the telephone now and Rick could feel the stiffness in the backs of his legs, the sharp tingling of his nerve ends. The enervating weakness that held him momentarily immobile came from the awful sense of helplessness as he understood what must inevitably happen.

For he knew Brainard had made up his mind and the decision was not based on reason but on the stubborn, uncompromising, and vindictive traits that had so often motivated his actions. But there was courage here, too, and the threat of the other gun did not seem to bother him. His thoughts, if he had any, must have been centered on what happened to his daughter as his groping fingers found the telephone.

Until then Rick had no plan, no ideas. He wanted only to stop the senseless tragedy he saw building and it finally came to him that there might be a way. Both he and Farrell were no more than innocent bystanders in this duel of wills. If he could step in front of Elinor he did not think she would shoot him, nor could Brainard fire at the woman.

He yelled something to get their attention. Then, with the perspiration drying coldly on his spine, he took his first step, but even then he saw he was too late.

Brainard picked up the telephone and Elinor was as good as her word. Ignoring Rick, she squeezed the trigger and the little automatic bucked in her hand. Almost simultaneously a heavier sound exploded in the room and Rick saw the slug strike the woman's chest and knock her back into the chair. Somewhere above Brainard's head the glass in a picture frame dissolved and fell with a tinkling sound to the carpet.

Brainard stood as he was, the telephone in one hand, the gun in the other. It was at once clear that he had not been hit and Rick never knew whether Elinor had missed because she had fired with her left hand or whether, sensing in the final instant that this was the best way out for her, she had missed deliberately.

In the moment of impact there was only a look of mild surprise on the face he had once thought so full of graciousness and courage and dignity. Slowly then, as the gun slipped from limp fingers and thudded to the floor, a slackness began to work on the features and the dark-blue eyes started to cloud. There was a small stain on the inside of the left breast and as he stared at it he heard the hoarse cry which tore at Farrell's throat as he pushed Rick aside and dropped to one knee beside his wife.

Rick swallowed hard and tried to close his mind against the things his eyes had seen. As he started for Brainard he understood that, ironically enough, the call which had been so important to the older man had never been made.

The instrument lay forgotten beside its pedestal. Brainard had dropped into the near-by chair, head down and the gun dangling loosely between his knees. He did not look up as Rick dialed the operator and said what he had to say about the police and a doctor.

When he hung up and glanced at Brainard he saw a crushed and beaten man as the shock of what he had done made itself felt. Reaction had erased for the time being the selfish and indomitable strains that had made him the man he was and Rick understood that, though justified, the memory of this night would remain with him forever.

"It was self-defense," he said, not looking up but still thinking of himself. "I gave her the first shot, didn't I? . . . H—how is she?" he said in a voice Rick could hardly hear.

Farrell was still on one knee beside his wife, his eyes wet and her hands in his. He was mumbling something about it being all right, and as she had so often done in the past, she cut him off.

"Yes," she said. "It will be all right, Austin. It is so much better this way." She coughed and her head sank lower before she whispered: "I'm sorry. You did all you could and if you have to go to prison for a while you will be paid. . . . I lied about my will. I didn't change it. It's all yours now and—"

Her voice trailed off and Rick could stand there no longer. He walked swiftly from the room and threw the front door wide open. He gulped air and tried to still the tremor in his legs. He forced his mind on while he waited for the first police car and somehow the image of his son appeared to quiet his thoughts.

He would have to find out about the funeral from Brainard but for now it was enough to know that the boy would not be hurt by what had happened tonight. At twelve, and so far away, there would be no permanent scar. And Nancy—

He stepped to the edge of the porch. As yet there was no sign of the police car and then, remembering his promise to call, he knew he had to talk to her before the inquisition began. He did not know just how he would begin or what he would say but it was terribly important that he hear her voice. Somewhere there would be another telephone in the house and now he turned and went back inside to look for it.